ESSENTIAL REPERTOIRE

FOR THE YOUNG CHOIR

BY
JANICE KILLIAN
MICHAEL O'HERN
LINDA RANN
EDITED BY
EMILY CROCKER

ISBN 0-7935-4338-X

HAL•LEONARD™
CORPORATION
7777 W. BLUEMOUND RD. P.O. BOX 13819 MILWAUKEE, WI 53213

AUTHORS

Dr. Janice Killian, Music Education
Texas Woman's University, Denton, Texas

Michael O'Hern, Choral Director
Lake Highlands Junior High
Richardson Independent School District, Texas

Linda Rann, Choral Director
Dan F. Long Middle School
Carrollton-Farmers Branch Independent School
District, Texas

PROJECT EDITOR
Emily Crocker
Director of Choral Publications
Hal Leonard Corporation, Milwaukee, Wisconsin

PRODUCTION EDITOR
Ryan French
Choral Editor
Hal Leonard Corporation, Milwaukee, Wisconsin

CONSULTANTS
Glenda Casey, Choral Director
Berkner High School
Richardson Independent School District, Texas

Bobbie Douglass, Choral Director
L. D. Bell High School
Hurst-Euless-Bedford Independent School District,
Texas

Jan Juneau, Choral Director
Klein High School
Klein Independent School District, Texas

Dr. John Leavitt, Composer and Conductor
Wichita, Kansas

Brad White, Choral Director
Richland High School
Birdville Independent School District, Texas

Printed in the United States of America

Send all inquiries to:
Hal Leonard Corporation
7777 W. Bluemound Rd., Box 13819
Milwaukee, WI 53213

CONTENTS

CONTENTS cont.

TO THE TEACHER

Why We Wrote This Book

We created this series because we are vitally committed to the nurturing of choral music, to the more effective teaching of choral music, and particularly to the encouragement of the young musicians who perform choral music. We believe that every child is musically expressive and deserves the opportunity to explore that capacity.

Too often, our definitions of literacy have been limited to words on paper. Although aspects of music can be taught as the written word (i.e., as a series of facts or as a written symbolic language), ultimately music is perhaps not best understood through the written word, but rather as a unique way of looking at the world, a special dimension of human understanding. What one understands, expresses, or feels when performing choral music is indeed "another way of knowing." We believe that it is vital that our children be given opportunities to experience this expanded literacy.

Janice Killian   **Michael O'Hern**   **Linda Rann**

About the Series

The four levels of *Essential Repertoire* (Young Choir, Developing Choir, Concert Choir, and Concert Choir - Artist Level) contain choral literature especially selected for choirs of differing ages and experience levels.

Level I, *Essential Repertoire for the Young Choir*, contains selections which take into account the limitations of the early adolescent voice. It contains musically accessible pieces which would be ideal for the beginning of the year, as well as selections appropriate for later in the year, or for groups which are ready for a special challenge. *Essential Repertoire for the Young Choir* is specifically designed for seventh and eighth graders, but the material included might be appropriate for any chorus, regardless of age.

Features of the Program

Each repertoire book contains a wide range of literature:

- a variety of historical periods
- a variety of other countries and cultures ;
- a mixture of English and foreign-language texts ;
- *both* • a variety of challenging and beginning level songs ;
- a mixture of styles: masterworks, folk songs and spirituals; a cappella and accompanied pieces; sacred and secular works, arrangements of familiar songs; and a few pop-style selections ,

Every effort was made to select high quality, time-tested literature.

Each song is independent of the others, i.e. there is no special sequence intended. Little prior knowledge is assumed on the part of the student. Teachers are encouraged to make selections as needed to create a varied and meaningful classroom and concert program.

Student information pages are included with each choral selection to help students learn basic musical skills, to be introduced to the cultural context in which the music was created and to evaluate their own progress.

The Teacher Editions contain the same information as the student text, plus much additional background information, as well as suggested lesson plans, vocal warm-ups, and performance tips.

The repertoire books are designed to be used in conjunction with *Essential Musicianship*, Book 1, a comprehensive choral method for teaching vocal technique, sight-singing, and music theory.

How to Use *Essential Repertoire for the Young Choir*

Each song is treated as an independent unit of study. Prior to each song is a page of information designed to be read by the student. Student pages consist of:

- Title and Composer, text information, and voicing/instrumentation.
- Cultural context of the song: Usually students can read and understand this section with limited guidance from the teacher.
- Musical terms: Students should be encouraged to find the listed terms in the song, and look up any unknown terms and/or symbols in the glossary.
- Preparation: Students will usually need teacher assistance in completing the Preparation section. This book is not designed to be student self-paced. Additional teaching suggestions, background information, and performance tips are included in the Teacher Edition.
- Evaluation: In most cases the Evaluation section is to be completed after the notes and rhythms of the piece have been mastered. Details for guiding the students' evaluation appear in the Teacher Edition.

Students should be encouraged to read the Cultural Context and Musical Terms sections of the text page prior to learning the song. This could be an effective activity for students while the teacher is involved in taking roll or other tasks. Students will usually need assistance in completing the rest of the text page.

The Teacher Edition

The Teacher Edition includes an extensive lesson plan for each choral selection which may be taught as suggested, expanded over a six-week period, or modified as needed. Each teaching plan contains the following:

- Student Text Page (slightly reduced in size)
- Ranges and song information (key, meter, form, performance possibilities)
- Learning objectives (Essential Elements) for each song correlated with the National Standards for Arts Education
- Historical/stylistic guidelines
- Answers to any student page questions
- Vocal technique/warm-ups/exercises
- Rehearsal guidelines and notes: 1) Suggested teaching sequence, and 2) Performance tips
- Evaluation suggestions for assessing student progress on the stated objectives
- Extension ideas

Who Should Use This Book

The authors of this text, all currently-practicing choral educators, bring a combined total of more than fifty years experience to the writing of this text. Their careful suggestions of tried and proven techniques provide a valuable resource of choral ideas for polishing performances.

Choral directors who are just entering the profession are encouraged to follow the suggested teaching sequence as written for each song to gain practical teaching skills.

Experienced choral directors may want to refer to the performance tips as a source of ideas for approaching a piece and refining it.

The warmups, vocalises, or polishing exercises included for every song in the Teacher Edition may be particularly applicable to a given song. They contain a wealth of ideas and suggestions which may be applied to other choral situations.

In Conclusion

Essential Repertoire for the Young Choir, when combined with the companion volume *Essential Musicianship*, is in essence, a complete curriculum for the choral experience — a core library of repertoire aimed at awakening the singer's potential for self development, musical expression, and personal esteem.

EFFECTIVE TEACHING CHECKLIST

Preparation:
- Good planning leads to a successful rehearsal.
- Establish high expectations from the start – students want to succeed.
- Establish a routine and basic standards of behavior – and stick to it!
- Follow your planned routine every rehearsal (e.g. opening cue that rehearsal has begun, warm-up, sight-reading, repertoire, evaluation). Younger choirs in particular respond well to structure in a rehearsal.
- Plan, plan, plan.
- Develop long-range planning (the entire year's goals and activities, the semester, the month) and short-range planning (weekly plans and the daily lesson as they fit within the entire year's goals).
- Vary teaching strategies: modeling, peer coaching, large group, small group, cooperative learning, individual instruction, student conductors, independent practice.
- Study the score well. Anticipate problem areas.
- Be able to sing any one part while playing another.
- Know the vocal ranges of each member of the chorus.
- Select appropriate music to fit those vocal ranges.
- Remember: Out-of-range results in out-of-tune singing.
- Select music of appropriate difficulty for the group.
- Plan evaluation techniques in advance.
- Have all necessary supplies and equipment ready (music in folders or ready to pass out, tapes cued, director's folder handy, recording equipment set, etc.) before the lesson begins.
- Plan to make beautiful music at least once during every rehearsal.

Presentation:
- Begin each lesson with aural activities (singing) rather than verbal activities (talking)
- Make all parts of the lesson musical – including warm-ups and sight-reading.
- Rehearse a cappella. Use the piano as little as possible.
- Remember: Delivering information is not necessarily teaching.
- Display a positive attitude.
- Communicate effectively and concisely.
- Enthusiasm is essential.
- Make learning an enjoyable experience.
- Respect legitimate effort on the part of every student.
- Be the best musician you can be.
- Laugh often.

Pacing:
- Be mentally thirty seconds ahead of the class at all times.
- Know where the lesson will lead before it happens.
- Vary activities and standing/sitting positions.
- Plan a smooth transition from one activity to the next.
- Avoid "lag" time.
- If a "teachable" moment occurs, make the most of it.
- Avoid belaboring any one exercise, phrase, activity – come back to it at another time.
- Always give students a reason for repeating a section.
- Provide at least one successful musical experience in every rehearsal.

Evaluation:
- Assess student learning in every lesson (formally or informally).
- Vary the assessment activities.
- Consider evaluating individual as well as group effort.
- Tape the rehearsals often (audio and/or video).
- Study the rehearsal tapes: 1) to discover where overlooked errors occur, 2) to assist in planning the next rehearsal, or 3) to share findings with the students.
- Provide students with opportunities to evaluate themselves.
- Teach critical listening to the students by asking specific students or a group of students to listen for a specific thing (balance of parts in the polyphonic section, a correct uniform vowel sound on a particular word or words, rise and fall of phrase, etc.).
- Constantly evaluate what's really happening. (We often hear what we want to hear!)
- Listen, listen, listen!

NATIONAL STANDARDS FOR ARTS EDUCATION
CHORAL PERFORMING GROUPS Grades 7-8
Essential Elements for Choir

The *National Standards for Arts Education* were developed by the Consortium of National Arts Education Associations under the guidance of the National Committee for Standards in the Arts. The Standards were prepared under a grant from the U. S. Department of Education, the National Endowment for the Arts, and the National Endowment for the Humanities.

Essential Musicianship, and the corresponding repertoire collections, *Essential Repertoire for the Young Choir (Mixed, Treble, Tenor Bass)*, are a part of the series *Essential Elements For Choir* and are based on these National Standards. In order to help teachers and students attain the National Standards, the authors of *Essential Elements For Choir* have developed related statements, more specific objectives, called *Essential Elements*.

By structuring this course of study around these Essential Elements and the corresponding National Standards, teachers and their students may begin to construct a vital relationship with the arts, and in so doing, as with any subject, approach this curriculum with discipline and study. The National Standards spell out what every young American should know about the arts, and the Essential Elements provide a framework for achieving these goals.

In the chart below, the National Standards (both *Content Standards* and *Achievement Standards*) are listed in **bold italic** typeface. The corresponding Essential Elements which are used in *Essential Musicianship* and *Essential Repertoire for the Young Choir* follow each National Standard in standard typeface. Throughout the text, each specific Essential Element is identified with the corresponding National Standard, i.e. *The student will sing with tall, uniform vowels (NS 1A).*

1. *SINGING ALONE AND WITH OTHERS, A VARIED REPERTOIRE OF MUSIC*
A. *Students sing accurately and with good breath control throughout their singing ranges, alone and in small and large ensembles.*

(1) Understand the vocal mechanism including parts and functions, and the changing voice
- The student will describe and demonstrate the posture, breathing, vowel placement, and articulation necessary for good singing tone.
- The student will develop an understanding of the vocal mechanism.
- The student will develop an understanding of the breathing mechanism.
- The student will build a repertoire of effective vocalises.

(2) Develop and use correct singing posture
- The student will describe and demonstrate good posture for singing.
- The student will develop the posture and breath control needed to support choral tone through sustained phrases.

(3) Develop and use correct breathing skills
- The student will develop the diaphragmatic breathing needed to support choral tone.
- The student will develop breathing techniques emphasizing the open throat.
- The student will develop breath control adequate for performing melismas, crescendos, and supporting sustained phrases.

(4) Develop good vocal tone, demonstrating proper breath support, vowel pronunciation, and placement/focus and head/chest voice
- The student will discuss and demonstrate head and chest voice.
- The student will discuss and demonstrate correct vowel pronunciation and tone placement.
- The student will develop the posture and breath control adequate for performing melismas, crescendos, and supporting sustained phrases.

(5) Develop proper diction through correct use of vowel shapes, syllabic stress, consonants, and diphthongs
- The student will sing with tall uniform vowels.
- The student will develop proper diction through the use of correct vowel shapes.
- The student will discuss and demonstrate the neutral vowel (schwa).
- The student will discuss and demonstrate the appropriate pronunciation of diphthongs.
- The student will develop good diction through the precise articulation of consonants.
- The student will articulate the "r" consonant correctly.
- The student will develop clear diction to convey the meaning of the text.

(6) Develop intonation awareness
- The student will aurally discriminate between in-tune and out-of-tune singing.
- The student will practice good intonation.
- The student will develop intonation awareness through the study of whole steps and half steps.
- The student will develop intonation awareness through the study of the chromatic scale.

(7) Exercise responsible use and care of the voice
- The student will develop technical singing skill focusing on the responsible use and care of the voice.
- The student will develop an appreciation of the care needed for responsible use of the voice.

B. Students sing with expression and technical accuracy a repertoire of vocal literature with a level of difficulty of 2 on a scale of 1-6 including some songs performed from memory.
(National Standard 1B applies only to non-performing groups.)

C. Students sing music representing diverse genres and cultures with expression appropriate for the work being performed.
- The student will develop proper Latin, French, German, Catalan, Hebrew, Italian, Spanish, and English diction through the correct use of vowel shapes and syllabic stress.
- The student will sing choral literature from Africa, Italy, France, Germany, Spain, Mexico, Israel, England, Ireland, Russia, Scotland, and the United States.
- The student will sing choral literature of various styles including spirituals, lullabies, folk songs from around the world, jazz, pop, and gospel, as well as traditional choral literature.
- The student will sing choral literature from various time periods including Renaissance, Baroque, Classical, Romantic, and the Twentieth Century.

D. Students sing music written in two and three parts.
- Students will sing choral literature written for unison, two-part, three-part, and four-part choruses.

E. Students sing with expression and technical accuracy a varied repertoire of vocal literature with a level of difficulty of 3, on a scale of 1-6, including some songs performed from memory.
(National Standard 1E applies to performing groups.)
<u>Performance Activities</u>
(1) The student will perform individually, in small ensembles, and in large groups
- The student will apply music reading skills to the performance of short accompanied or a cappella songs.
- The student will perform in small ensembles for the choir, and where appropriate, for a wider audience.
- The student will have the opportunity to perform solos, if desired.

(2) Articulating and practicing proper concert etiquette
- The student will describe and demonstrate proper concert etiquette.

(3) Performance literature
- The student will perform choral literature identified by such state and national organizations as the American Choral Directors Association, Music Educators National Conference, the Texas University Interscholastic League, the New York State School Music Association, the Wisconsin Music Educators Association, and others, as being of appropriate quality and difficulty for this age group.
<u>Choral Ensemble Techniques</u>

(4) Sing in tune through tone-vowel placement and careful listening
  - The student will increase his/her ability to sing in tune while singing harmony.
  - The student will improve intonation through the use of blended, supported vowels.
  - The student will listen carefully to rehearsal recordings, identifying areas of intonation weaknesses.

(5) Blend with other ensemble voices in areas of tone quality, diction, and intonation
  - The student will demonstrate the ability to blend with other ensemble voices utilizing appropriate tone quality, diction, and intonation.
  - The student will listen carefully to rehearsal recordings, identifying areas in which blend needs improvement.

(6) Respond to conducting
  - The student will respond appropriately to conducting.
  - The student will view rehearsal videotapes, noticing areas in which all ensemble members are not responding to conducting gestures.

(7) Pitch and rhythm accuracy
  - The student will develop rhythmic accuracy by dividing the beat.
  - The student will hold long notes for full value.
  - The student will perform rhythms, syncopated rhythms, and changing meters with understanding and accuracy.
  - The student will aurally identify areas in which pitch accuracy needs improvement and will attempt to repair those sections of music.
  - The student will develop pitch accuracy over time through repeated practice.

(8) Demonstrate style characteristics (historical period, culture, dynamics, composer intent)
  - The student will perform dynamic and tempo changes as indicated by the composer.
  - The student will develop choral performance techniques of the Renaissance, Baroque, Classical, Romantic, and Twentieth Century eras.
  - The student will become familiar with the musical terms which appear in each of the songs studied.

(9) Demonstrate phrasing (shape, movement)
  - The student will aurally discriminate between musical and unmusical phrases.
  - The student will develop the ability to musically shape a phrase.
  - The student will demonstrate the ability to sing long sustained phrases while maintaining pitch accuracy.

(10) Demonstrate textual clarity (word accent, syllabic stress)
  - The student will aurally discriminate between appropriate and inappropriate word stress.
  - The student will demonstrate the ability to sing with appropriate syllabic stress.

(11) Demonstrate expression (sensitivity, mood, physical indication of feeling)
  - The student will sing expressively as indicated by appropriate facial expression.
  - The student will physically express sensitivity to the text.
  - The student will verbalize the meaning of the text.

2. PERFORMING ON INSTRUMENTS, ALONE AND WITH OTHERS, A VARIED REPERTOIRE OF MUSIC

It is the purpose of this course in choral performance to emphasize the development of the voice and the choral art. Therefore, instrumental performance is beyond the scope of this text. It should be noted, however, that skill on a musical instrument, particularly a keyboard, is a definite asset for a singer/chorister and such skill should be encouraged at every opportunity. Choral directors should consider such choral and instrumental combinations as:
  - Using student pianists as rehearsal and/or performance accompanists.
  - Using instrumental accompaniments played by students.
  - Highlighting instrumentalists from within the chorus on appropriate programs.
  - Arranging joint band/orchestra/choir performances whenever possible.

3. IMPROVISING MELODIES, VARIATIONS, AND ACCOMPANIMENTS

A. Students improvise simple harmonic accompaniments.

(1) The student will improvise a harmonic accompaniment to the reading of a specified poem using an autoharp or other chordal instrument.

(2) The student will accompany an ensemble on guitar, autoharp or keyboard.

B. Students improvise melodic embellishments and simple rhythmic and melodic variations on given pentatonic melodies and melodies in major keys.

(1) The student will improvise short melodies in C pentatonic on Orff instruments.

(2) The student will improvise a pentatonic piece with contrasting sections.

(3) The student will improvise pentatonic melodies using deliberate dynamic contrasts.

C. Students improvise short melodies, unaccompanied, and over given rhythmic accompaniments, each in a consistent style, meter, and tonality.

(1) The student will improvise short melodies over rhythmic patterns played on classroom instruments.

(2) The student will improvise on a given syncopated rhythmic pattern.

4. COMPOSING AND ARRANGING MUSIC WITHIN SPECIFIED GUIDELINES

A. Students compose short pieces within specified guidelines, demonstrating how the elements of music are used to achieve unity and variety, tension and release, and balance.

(1) The student will compose rhythm exercises of quarter, half, and whole note patterns.

(2) The student will compose a short composition in 2/4, 3/4, or 4/4 meter.

(3) The student will create a musical composition using contrasting sections.

(4) The student will compose and perform a rhythm piece.

B. Students arrange simple pieces for voices or instruments other than those for which the pieces were written.

(1) The student will arrange a nursery rhyme or other familiar poem for speech chorus.

(2) The student will compose a rhythmic setting for a tongue twister and arrange it for speech chorus and classroom instruments.

(3) The student will arrange familiar folk or patriotic songs into a medley.

(4) The student will arrange a familiar song in a contrasting style (e.g. from traditional to swing style).

C. Students use a variety of traditional and nontraditional sound sources and electronic media when composing and arranging.

(1) The student will use music notation softward to notate a C major scale.

(2) Students will create musical compositions on poetry by [Robert Lewis Stevenson] using computer generated sound or other musical sources.

(3) Students will compose brief compositions using sounds available in the classroom.

5. READING AND NOTATING MUSIC

A. Students will read whole, half, quarter, eighth, sixteenth, and dotted notes and rests in 2/4, 3/4, 4/4, 6/8, 3/8, and alle breve meter signatures.

(1) Read, write and perform rhythm patterns

• The student will discriminate between beat and rhythm.

• The student will echo-sing/chant/clap rhythmic patterns.

• The student will read and perform quarter, half, whole, eighth note, and rest rhythms accurately.

• The student will write quarter, half, whole, eighth note, and rest rhythms accurately.

• The student will read and perform rhythm patterns in various meters.

• The student will read and perform rhythms in changing meter.

B. Students read at sight simple melodies in both the treble and bass clefs.

(1) Read and sing melodic patterns and harmonic structures in a variety of keys and tonalities, using specific methodology such as solfege or numbers

• The student will read and sing rhythmic and melodic patterns in treble and bass clefs.

• The student will read chord patterns in the keys of C, F, and G major in treble and bass clefs.

• The student will read and sing melodic patterns using the tonic, dominant, and subdominant chords in treble and bass clefs.

• The student will apply knowledge of whole and half steps.

C. Students identify and define standard notation symbols for pitch, rhythm, dynamics, tempo, articulation, and expression.

(1) Demonstrate knowledge of music theory including conventional and unconventional notation
- The student will recognize and apply basic rhythmic notation (whole, half, quarter, eighth, and dotted notes and rests).
- The student will recognize and apply knowledge of basic pitch notation (grand staff, pitch names, clefs, sharps, flats, and naturals).
- The student will recognize and apply key signatures.

(2) Demonstrate knowledge of music theory by using music terminology
- The student will become familiar with the musical terms found in specific songs included in the student texts.
- The student will perform a piece of music utilizing the musical terminology indicated in the music to interpret the piece as suggested by the composer.

D. Students use standard notation to record their musical ideas and the musical ideas of others.

(1) Learn and use grandstaff, key and time signatures, pitch and rhythm notation
- The student will describe and review elements of musical notation.
- The student will recognize and apply basic rhythmic notation (whole, half, quarter, eighth, and dotted rhythms and rests).
- The student will recognize and apply basic pitch notation (grand staff, pitch names, clefs, sharp, flat and natural).
- The student will define pitch, scale, and key.
- The student will recognize and apply key signatures.

(2) Learn and use scale systems, key relationships, and chord progressions
- The student will describe the triad and the tonic chord.
- The student will sing and recognize whole and half steps in major scales.
- The student will describe and recognize intervals, chords, and triads.
- The student will describe the concepts of measure, barline, and meter.

(3) Recognize musical forms
- The singer will recognize and discuss musical forms, including: ABA, strophic, variation and coda.
- The student will recognize and perform a musical example of canonic form.
- The student will recognize form through repetition and contrast of musical material.

E. Students sight-read, accurately and expressively, music with a level of difficulty of 2 on a scale of 1-6.
(Applies to performing classes only)

(1) Sing and recognize intervals
- The student will recognize and perform melodic and harmonic intervals.
- The student will sight-read exercises which emphasize the tonic chord.
- The student will recognize and perform harmonic intervals in an ensemble.
- The student will practice singing melodic intervals in a short a cappella song.
- The student will describe and recognize intervals, chords, and triads.

(2) Read and sing melodic patterns and harmonic structures in a variety of keys and tonalities, using specific methodology such as solfege or numbers
- The student will sight-read short unison a cappella pieces.
- The student will sight-read short accompanied unison pieces.
- The student will sight-read short accompanied two-, three-, and four-part songs in the keys of C, F, and G major.
- The student will sight-read short a cappella two-, three-, and four-part songs in the keys of C, F, and G major.

6. LISTENING TO, ANALYZING, AND DESCRIBING MUSIC

A. Students describe specific musical events in a given aural example, using appropriate terminology.

(1) The student will listen to a recording and describe the musical events in a specified choral work using the terminology with which he/she is presently working (e.g., describe the polyphonic entrances of soprano, alto, tenor and bass; aurally discriminate between examples of monophony, homophony and polyphony).

(2) The student will use appropriate terminology to describe recordings of his/her own performances.

B. Students analyze the uses of elements of music in aural examples representing diverse genres and cultures.

(1) The student will compare and contrast diverse types of choral music techniques (e.g. jazz tone quality vs. Renaissance tone quality, or dynamic contrasts in spirituals vs. that of the Baroque).

(2) The student will compare and contrast tone quality among diverse musical types such as traditional choral music, gospel music, country-western groups, ensemble music of China, and that of the Middle East.

(3) The student will discuss and analyze the musical characteristics of a madrigal, spiritual, or American folk song.

C. Students demonstrate knowledge of the basic principles of meter, rhythm, tonality, intervals, chords, and harmonic progressions in their analyses of music.

(1) The student will discuss musical elements, including meter and rhythm, present in a recording of choral music.

(2) The student will discuss musical elements, including tonality, melodic and harmonic intervals, and harmonic progressions of I, IV, and V.

7. EVALUATING MUSIC AND MUSIC PERFORMANCES

A. Students develop criteria for evaluating the quality and effectiveness of music performances and compositions and apply the criteria in their personal listening and performing.

(1) Critical Evaluation: Monitoring progress toward musical goals
- The student will monitor progress toward musical goals by noting development of his/her individual range.
- The student will monitor progress toward a musical goal by listening to early and more recent rehearsal recordings to note improvement in such choral techniques as intonation, vowel shapes, balance, and blend of the ensemble.

(2) Critical Evaluation: Evaluate self both as a solo and ensemble performer
- The student will listen critically to self and the chorus, concentrating on the balance and blend of the voice parts.

(3) Critical Evaluation: Evaluate self and others' solo and group rehearsals and/or performances
- The student will evaluate self as a solo performer by taping himself/herself singing at the end of the year as compared with the beginning of the year.
- The student will evaluate progress as an ensemble performer by listening critically to tapes, comparing polished performances with early rehearsals of a specific work.

(4) Citizenship Through Group Endeavor: Working effectively as a responsible team member
- The student will work effectively with others as a responsible team member by performing in small ensembles, creating original choreography in groups, and supporting efforts of the group through suggestions, encouragement, and enthusiasm.

(5) Citizenship Through Group Endeavor: Developing leadership abilities
* The student will develop leadership abilities by serving as student director, designing and teaching original choreography, leading a small ensemble, and acting as a section leader during rehearsal and/or sight-reading sessions.

B. Students evaluate the quality and effectiveness of their own and others' performances, compositions, arrangements, and improvisations by applying specific criteria appropriate for the style of the music and offer constructive suggestions for improvement.
(1) Evaluate own and others' solo and group rehearsals and/or performances
* The student will evaluate his own and other's solo and group rehearsals and/or performances.
* The student will listen critically to self and the chorus, concentrating on the balance and blend of the voice parts.
* The student will listen critically to self and the chorus, concentrating on such choral techniques as intonation, diction, memorization, uniform vowels, and choral tone quality.
* The student will evaluate progress as an ensemble performer by listening critically to tapes comparing polished performances with early rehearsals of a specific work.

8. UNDERSTANDING RELATIONSHIPS BETWEEN MUSIC, THE OTHER ARTS, AND DISCIPLINES OUTSIDE THE ARTS

A. Students compare, in two or more arts, how the characteristic materials of each art can be used to transform similar events, scenes, emotions, or ideas into works of art.
(1) The student will translate monophonic movement in music into monophonic movement in visual art or dance.

(2) The student will combine history, drama, and music for an in-class presentation.

(3) The student will combine the art forms of drama and music.

(4) The student will combine drama, poetry, dance, and music to create a Shakespearean scene.

B. Students describe ways in which the principles and subject matter of other disciplines taught in the school are interrelated with those of music.
(1) The student will relate a song based on the poetry of [Christina Rossetti] to language arts.

(2) The student will apply language arts skills during music classes by listing different words which mean [pitch].

(3) The student will apply information learned in music [anatomy of the breathing mechanism] to science classes.

(4) The student will describe poetic imagery in a song.

(5) The student will relate information about the ears, nose, and throat to issues of voice production and vocal health.

(6) The student will relate music performed in class with events in American and world history.

9. UNDERSTANDING MUSIC IN RELATION TO HISTORY AND CULTURE

A. Students describe distinguishing characteristics of representative music genres and styles from a variety of cultures.
(1) Hearing, identifying, describing, and performing music from a variety of musical styles, eras, and composers.
* The student will develop an understanding of the Western choral tradition, American spirituals, international folk songs, American jazz style, and the choral music of various countries through discussion, listening, and performance.
* The student will learn to sing in a variety of styles, (i.e. legato, jazz swing, Renaissance tone quality vs. Romantic tone quality, etc.).

(2) Recognizing similarities and differences between choral styles of the major historical periods
  • The student will recognize and describe similarities and differences among choral styles of the past and present.
  • The student will perform literature and discuss characteristics of the Renaissance, Baroque, Classical, Romantic, and Twentieth Century eras.

B. Students classify by genre, style, historical period, composer, and title a varied body of exemplary musical works and explain the characteristics that cause each work to be considered exemplary.
  (1) Recognizing similarities and differences between choral styles of the major historical periods
  • The student will recognize and describe similarities and differences among choral styles of the past and present.
  • The student will perform literature and discuss characteristics of the Renaissance, Baroque, Classical, Romantic, and Twentieth Century eras.
  • The student will perform dynamic and tempo changes as indicated by the composer.
  • The student will identify geographic regions and discuss the music from those regions.
  • The student will compare and contrast music today with music of 400 years ago.
  • The student will research music sung by persons of his/her grandparents' generation.
  • The student will write an essay comparing popular songs of today with those of the Renaissance.

C. Students compare, in several cultures of the world, functions music serves, roles of musicians, and conditions under which music is typically performed.
  (1) The student will explore careers in the field of music.

  (2) The student will research (through books, video, and other media) the role of musicians around the world.

  (3) The student will study how music is used in various cultures by researching, discussing, and, where appropriate, demonstrating a specified time or place (colonial America, African folk song, etc.).

AURA LEE

Composer: George R. Poulton, arranged by Emily Crocker

Text: W.W. Fosdick

Voicing: TB

Key: B♭
Meter: 4/4
Form: Strophic with coda
Style: Lyric Folk Song
Accompaniment: Piano, optional a cappella

Programming: Concert or festival, Civil War or Americana theme program

Ranges:

Student Book Page 1

AURA LEE

Composer: George R. Poulton, arranged by Emily Crocker
Text: W.W. Fosdick
Voicing: TB (optional a cappella)

Cultural Context:
The song "Aura Lee" was written by W.W. Fosdick (lyrics) and George R. Poulton (music) in 1861. During the American Civil War it was a favorite of the Union Army. Reportedly, it was sung by the graduation class at West Point in 1865 with new words and the title "Army Blue."

Almost 100 years later in 1956, Vera Matson borrowed the melody with a new set of words for singing legend Elvis Presley. It became the song "Love Me Tender" which was the first record in history to get advanced sales of 1,000,000 copies.

Musical Terms:
(♩ = ca.84) *mp* (mezzo forte) (crescendo)

mf (mezzo forte) (decrescendo) *rit.* (ritardando)

⁀ (fermata) ' (breath mark) harmony

a tempo *p* (piano) ⁻ (tenuto)

melody

Preparation:
Maintaining balance between melody and harmony is important in good choral singing. In this arrangement both Tenor and Baritone have an opportunity to sing melody and harmony.

Verse 1/Chorus:	Tenor and Baritone sing melody
Verse 2:	Tenor sings harmony; Baritone sings melody
Chorus:	Tenor sings melody; Baritone sings harmony
Verse 3:	Tenor and Baritone sing melody
Chorus:	Tenor sings melody; Baritone sings harmony

Look through your music and mark your part by writing "m" above your part when you sing melody and "h" above your part when you sing harmony.

Evaluation:
As you listen to your choir singing this song, check for the following:

• Is there balance between melody and harmony?

• Is one part overpowered by another?

(Answers to questions on student page)
Preparation: Mark melody (m) and harmony (h) for Tenor and Baritone parts as follows:

mm. 5-20	*T=m; B=m*
mm. 21-28	*T=h; B=m*
mm. 29-36	*T=m; B=h*
mm. 37-44	*T=m; B=m*
mm. 45-52	*T=m; B=h*

Objectives:
- The student will listen critically as a participating member of an ensemble, concentrating on the balance of the voice parts. (*National Standard* 7A, 7B)
- The student will learn to sing in a smooth legato style. (*NS* 5C, 5D)

Historical/Stylistic Guidelines:
Review the material found in the Cultural Context section of the student page. Two additional facts are:

Emily Crocker, currently Director of Choral Publications for Hal Leonard Corporation, taught public school music in Texas for fifteen years. She has earned degrees from North Texas State University (now University of North Texas) and Texas Woman's University. Ms. Crocker has published over one hundred choral pieces.

This lyrical piece is an excellent teaching tool for legato musical line, beautiful tone quality, phrasing, blend and balance. It will be a favorite with the singers and audience alike.

Vocal Technique/Warm-Ups/Exercises:
Smooth legato singing is required to interpret this song correctly. To create a legato line with pure vowels practice the following (copy onto board, overhead projector, or handout). Sustained breath support is essential to legato singing. Perform each exercise on one continuous breath.

Explanation:
- Speak through line on an "s" sound to feel a steady stream of air throughout the phrase.
- Sing on an "oo" vowel for a smooth line maintaining the steady stream of air.
- Sing only the vowel of the text with "n" in front. Remind singers of steady air, smooth line and pure vowels.
- Sing the melody with text, thinking the vowel sound.

Rehearsal Guidelines and Notes
Suggested Sequence:
1. Familiarize students with the musical terms found in this piece as listed in the student text. (NS 5C)
2. Review the material found in the Preparation section of the student page. Have students mark their music accordingly.
3. Teach all of the melody sections on a neutral syllable (or use them as a sight reading exercise).
4. Teach all of the harmony sections on a neutral syllable (or use them as a sight reading exercise).
5. Phrasing is the key to this piece:

  - Shape each phrase with a crescendo and decrescendo.
  - Locate the important words in the phrase. Stress these more than others.
  - Make each phrase as musical, lyrical and flowing as possible.
  - Then add the dynamic markings as indicated in the score.

Performance Tips:

- Ask the singers to sing only the notes within their ranges. If a part is too high or too low for their natural range, have them mouth the words and resume singing when back in their range. They may want to circle the notes in their music that they should not sing.
- Keep the tone light and forward. Baritones may have a tendency to "swallow" their sound or oversing. Ask the baritones to "place the sound" right behind their front teeth.
- Remind the singers to drop and relax the jaw, and to bring the corners of their mouth inward.
- Breath support is the key to good tone and legato singing.
- Create a rise and fall in each phrase.
- Beware the E-naturals in the Tenor I part at m. 22 and m. 26. Remind the tenors to think high as they sing these pitches. The tendency is to sing closer to an E-flat as indicated in the key signature.
- This piece would work well for a small ensemble.

Evaluation:

Complete the Evaluation section of the student page. Direct the students to look at their music as they listen to the tape. Mark the measures where the balance could be improved. (*NS 7A, 7B*)

Extension:

Obtain a recording of Elvis Presley's "Love Me Tender." Ask students to compare and contrast the two versions.

Aura Lee

For TB a cappella or with Piano

This piece can be performed in a number of ways. It may be sung a cappella or accompanied. At meas. 21, the baritone may either sing the lyrics, or "oo." If range is a problem, the cued baritone notes in measures 13-20 are optional. In other places, the choir may sing the cued notes to provide fuller harmony.

Music by GEORGE R. POULTON
Arranged by EMILY CROCKER

Words by W.W. FOSDICK

Student
Book Page
3

swal - lows in the air.   In thy blush the

In   thy   blush   the
(Opt.) Oo

rose was _ born,   mu - sic   when   you _ spake.

rose   was   born,   mu - sic   when   you   spake.

Through thine a - zure   eyes   the _ moon,   spark-ling seemed to

Through   thine   a - zure   eyes   the   moon,   spark - ling   seemed to

Student Book Page 4

break, to ___ break. Au - ra Lee, Au - ra Lee,

break.

birds of crim - son wing nev - er song have

sung to me as in that bright, sweet spring.

Student Book Page 5

Au - ra Lee, take my gold - en ring.

Love and light re - turn with thee, and swal - lows with the

rit. *p*

spring. Au - ra Lee!

Student Book Page 7

BLOW YE WINDS

Composer: Sea Chantey,
  arranged by Emily Crocker
Text: Traditional
Voicing: TTB

Key: B♭/F major
Meter: ¢
Form: Strophic with introduction
  and coda
Style: Sea Chantey

Accompaniment: Piano
Programming: Concert or festival,
  Americana program

Ranges:

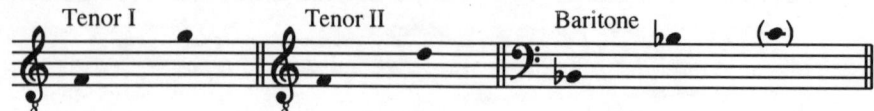

Student Book Page 8

BLOW YE WINDS

Composer: Sea Chantey, arranged by Emily Crocker
Text: Traditional
Voicing: TTB

Cultural Context:

"Blow Ye Winds" is an example of a sea *chantey*. Life was hard on the sea. To seemingly lighten the work load and raise their spirits, the sailors sang while working. They also sang sea chanteys for relaxation and entertainment. Often a leader would set the tempo and sing the introductory verses and the rest of the crew joined on the chorus. "Blow Ye Winds," a ballad about whaling ships and their crews, tells how it was advertised in Boston, New York, and Buffalo for 500 American Sailors. Once out to sea, half were sick on deck and the other half down below!

Musical Terms:

(♩ = ca. 100)   *mf* (mezzo forte)   *f* (forte)

     (crescendo)   *p* (piano)

Preparation:

Clear articulation is essential for the success of "Blow Ye Winds." Recite these words distinctly. To improve your articulation try to exaggerate the consonants and the movement of your mouth.

'Tis advertised in Boston, New York and Buffalo,
Five hundred brave Americans a sailing for to go.

They send you to New Bedford, that famous sailing port.
And say you'll make five thousand miles before you're six months out.

Singing blow ye winds in the morning, blow ye winds high-o!
Clear away your running gear and blow ye winds high-o!

And now we're out to sea, my boys, the wind comes on to blow,
When half the watch is sick on deck, the other half below—

Singing blow ye winds in the morning, blow ye winds high-o!
Clear away your running gear and blow ye winds high-o!

Evaluation:

- Work with a partner chanting the text until all words are precise and clear. Recite the lines for each other, stressing clear and precise diction. Exaggerate the pronunciations of the words.

- Can you identify other sea chanteys found in this text?

Objectives:

- The student will sing with energy and clear diction. (*National Standard* 1A)
- The student will develop an understanding of the American sea chantey through discussion and performance. (*NS* 6B, 9A)

Historical/Stylistic Guidelines:

David Ewen in *All the Years of American Popular Music* (p. 29) classified the sea chantey into four categories: short haul, halliar, capstan, and fo'c'sle. The fo'c'sle chanteys (a derivative of forecastle - the ship's upper deck where the men lived and played) were sung for relaxation and entertainment, often accompanied by a violin, a harmonica or an accordion. A leader would usually set the tempo and sing the introductory verses, and the rest of the crew joined in on the chorus. "Blow Ye Winds," a ballad about whaling ships and their crews, is an example of a fo'c'sle chantey.

Vocal Technique/Warm-Ups/Exercises:

- Review the material found in the Preparation section of the student page to practice diction and clarity of text.
- Articulation is the action of the lips, teeth and tip of the tongue in making sounds. Remind students that singing is exaggerated speech. Practice the following exercise to enforce the importance of good articulation.

Lips,   teeth,   tip of the tongue,   Lips,   teeth,   tip of the tongue.

Repeat exercises up by half steps.

Rehearsal Guidelines and Notes
Suggested Sequence:

1. Familiarize students with the musical terms found in this piece as listed in the student text. (*NS* 5C)
2. Begin with the choruses of this song (mm. 17-24, mm. 33-40, mm. 49-56). Lead students to find similarities and differences in their own part among the three versions of the chorus. All three are slightly different. Teach each part separately, then combine parts.
3. Rehearse the three choruses in parts.
4. Shift attention to the three verses (mm. 9-16, mm. 25-32, mm. 41-48). Teach verse one and three first since they are the same, then teach the second verse.
5. Rehearse the three verses in parts.
6. Now try singing verse one and chorus. Correct any errors in pitch or rhythm. Proceed to verse two and chorus, then verse three and chorus checking for and correcting any errors.
7. Teach the introduction and coda last (mm. 4-8 and mm. 57-60).
8. Identify the sections that need re-teaching. Re-teach.
9. Finally sing the entire song utilizing all markings as indicated in the score.

Performance Tips:

- To maintain a pure vowel sound on the words "way," "hey," "away" remind students to think the vowel sound "eh" when singing these words. Keep the corners of the mouth in and the jaw dropped.
- Emphasize clear articulation on the three verses so the audience can hear and understand the story line.
- Teach the song a cappella for security in parts and tuning. Add the piano accompaniment last.

Evaluation:

- Lead students to practice the articulation exercise with a partner as explained in the Evaluation section of the student page. Ask the partners to select one student who articulates extremely well. Invite the selected students to demonstrate for the class (speaking the words). (*NS* 7A, 7B)
- To check for accuracy in parts, direct one section to sing the entire song alone, while the others listen for accuracy of pitch, rhythm and articulation. Repeat the process for the other sections. (*NS* 7A, 7B)

Blow Ye Winds

For TTB and Piano

Traditional Sea Chantey
Arranged by EMILY CROCKER

Student
Book Page
10

14

Student
Book Page
12

18

Clear a-way your run-ning gear and blow ye winds _____ high-

Clear a-way your run-ning gear and blow, blow ye winds,

Clear a-way your run-ning gear and blow, blow ye winds,

o! _____ Way hey, heave a - way!

blow ye winds in the morn - ing. Way hey! _____ High - o!

blow ye winds in the morn - ing. Way hey! _____ High - o!

19

THE BLUE AND THE GRAY

Composer: Civil War Songs,
arranged by Linda Spevacek
Text: Traditional
Voicing: TTB

Key: B♭ Major
Meter: 4/4
Form: Medley
Style: American Folk Song
Accompaniment: Piano

Programming: Concert, patriotic;
many opportunities for unison or
solo singing

Ranges:

THE BLUE AND THE GRAY

Composer: Civil War Songs, arranged by Linda Spevacek
Text: Traditional
Voicing: TTB

Student
Book Page
17

Cultural Context:
The Civil War was one of the most painful periods of our nation's history, leaving scars even today. "The Blue and the Gray" is a medley of songs from this period, reflecting the thoughts and feelings of both sides. The medley includes "Dixie" (song of the Confederacy), and "The Battle Cry of Freedom" and "Tramp, Tramp, Tramp" (both songs of the Union). The medley ends with a call to unify the country once again by rallying round the flag "shouting the battle cry of freedom."

Musical Terms:
(♩ = 108)   *mf* (mezzo forte)   *f* (forte)

unison   *ff* (fortissimo)

Preparation:
Although some of these songs may be familiar to you, be sure to sing the rhythms exactly as the arranger intended. The following exercise will help you with this challenge.

1. Tap the rhythm of this exercise. Make an obvious difference between ♫, ♪♩ and ♪ ♪ patterns.

2. Speak the words in rhythm.

3. Find other parts of "The Blue and the Gray" which have these rhythm patterns.

Evaluation:
Throughout history, each side in a battle has had its own songs. This medley presents songs from both sides of the Civil War. Write an essay about why you think people make up songs when they go to war. Do the songs make them feel better during a tragic time? Do the songs inspire them to fight harder? What other reasons could there be? For a different viewpoint about the songs of war, read the words to another song in your text, "My Johnny's a Soldier."

Objectives:

- The student will develop rhythmic accuracy and expand rhythmic reading skills, especially as related to dotted eighth and sixteenth patterns. (*National Standard* 1E)
- The student will perform patriotic choral literature. (*NS* 1E)

Historical/Stylistic Guidelines:

Daniel D. Emmett (1815-1904) of Mount Vernon, Ohio, composed "Dixie" in 1859. Other familiar Emmett compositions include: "Old Dan Tucker" (1843), "De Boatman's Dance" (1843), and "Blue Tail Fly" or "Jim Crack Corn" (1846). He was a member of the fife and drum corps in the Union army during the Civil War, stationed in Kentucky and Missouri. By 1895 he was a sensation in the southern states when he performed his own song, "Dixie."

"Dixie" was originally written as a "walk-around," a number in a minstrel show. Shortly thereafter it was played by the band for the inauguration of Jefferson Davis as Confederate president in 1861. Soon "Dixie" was the unofficial anthem of the Confederacy.

George Root (1820-1895) was a teacher and close associate of Lowell Mason in Boston. He went to New York City in 1844 as a musical instructor at the New York Institution for the Blind. From there he moved to Chicago in 1859 and joined the firm of Root and Cady, Chicago music publishers, where he composed the first published Civil War song, "The First Gun Is Fired," in 1861. He composed numerous other Civil War songs including "The Battle Cry of Freedom" or "Rally 'Round the Flag Boys" in 1863 and "Tramp, Tramp, Tramp" in 1864.

Vocal Technique/Warm-Ups/Exercises:

- Practice the rhythm drills on the student page Preparation section.
- Practice the following exercise (based on mm. 27-30) to emphasize tuning in three-part harmony.

    - Hold each chord until it tunes.
    - Sing on a neutral syllable.

Rehearsal Guidelines and Notes
Suggested Sequence:

1. Familiarize students with the musical terms found in this piece as listed in the student text. (*NS* 5C)
2. Teach each song of the medley as a separate unit.
3. Learn the rhythms for "Dixie," encouraging the singers to read the rhythms as written rather than as they have learned the song in the past.
4. Sing the familiar pitches (mm. 1-18) using the rhythms as notated in the score.
5. Prepare students for "Rally Round the Flag" by reviewing the Preparation on the student page.
6. Follow the same procedure for the other songs of the medley. "Rally 'Round the Flag" (starting m. 19) and "Tramp, Tramp, Tramp" (m. 37) may not be as familiar and more time may be spent teaching the pitches as well as the rhythms of those songs.
7. Use the exercise in the Vocal Technique section above to introduce three-part harmony (m. 27). Directors might consider making a similar exercise (isolating pitches from rhythm) for the last phrase (mm. 53-56).
8. Rehearse the entire song, paying particular attention to the dynamics indicated in the score.

Performance Tips:

- Remind singers not to slide between notes in such areas as "Hoo-ray!" (mm. 11-12).

- Pay special attention to m. 15 because it is the first instance of harmony. Inexperienced singers performing a familiar song may be tempted to keep singing the melody rather than the harmony.

- Remind students to stress the appropriate syllable and avoid gasping at the ends of phrases in such places as mm. 21-22 (SHOUTing the battle cry of FREEdom).

- Sing with an energetic, accented tone, but remind boys not to oversing and make a harsh, unpleasant tone. Boys with changing voices may not have the control to sing loudly. Good tone and accurate intonation may suffer with oversinging.

- Pay particular attention to finding appropriate ranges for every singer in the choir.

  OUT OF RANGE = OUT OF TUNE.

  - Remind basses to sing very lightly on the high D's (as in m. 5). Consider making this section a solo or adding Tenor II's on the higher notes.
  - Consider adding Basses to the Tenor II part on the low D's (m. 21).
  - Consider having Tenor I's mouth the words which are out of range (for example on the low G's mm. 31-32).

  - Note: All these suggestions depend on the individual singers and where they are in their voice change. Check individual ranges frequently (at least once a month or whenever a singer requests to be heard).

- Emphasize dynamic contrasts for a musical performance of this medley.

Evaluation:

- Read and discuss the Evaluation listed on the student page. (NS 7A, 7B)

- Record the rehearsal frequently, paying special attention to the section with harmony. Ask singers to listen critically for out-of-tune areas. (NS 7A, 7B)

Extension:

- This medley is an excellent way to feature the characteristics of the three different voice parts.

  - Listen to each student sing a scale to determine the extremes of his range. Encourage extreme high ranges as well as low pitches.
  - Notate each singer's range on a staff large enough to put on the wall. You will probably need a grand staff because it is likely that many of the boys' ranges will be well into the treble clef.
  - Periodically re-test the ranges and change the wall chart.
  - You may want to test girls' ranges also. Both male and female singers enjoy comparing their voices with those of their peers.

- Suggest that students collect other familiar patriotic songs and combine them into a medley using "Blue and the Gray" as a model. (NS 4A)

A Civil War medley including: Dixie, The Battle Cry For Freedom, and Tramp, Tramp, Tramp.

The Blue And The Gray

For TTB and Piano

Arranged by
LINDA SPEVACEK

Student
Book Page
18

* All voices may join at this point to form a unison chorus.

shout - ing the bat - tle cry of free - dom._____

shout - ing the bat - tle cry of free - dom._____

Tramp, tramp, tramp, the boys are march - ing,

Tramp, tramp, tramp, the boys are march - ing,

cheer up com-rades they will come.   And be-neath the star - ry flag   we shall

(Melody)

cheer up com-rades they will come.   And be - neath the star - ry flag   we shall

breathe the air a - gain of the free - land in our own be - lov - ed

breathe the air a - gain of the free - land in our own be - lov - ed

home. The Un - ion for - ev - er, hur - rah, boys, hur -rah!

home. The Un - ion for - ev - er, hur - rah, boys, hur -rah!

Down with the Trait - or and up with the Star. While we

Down with the Trait - or and up with the Star. While we

ral - ly 'round the flag, boys, we'll ral -ly once a - gain,

ral - ly 'round the flag, boys we'll ral -ly once a - gain, shout - ing the bat -tle cry,

R.H. (opt.)

52

T II   T I & II *f*

f

shout - ing the bat -tle cry, shout - ing the bat -tle cry of free -

shout - ing the bat - tle cry, shout - ing the bat -tle cry of free -

52

ff

dom! _____

ff

dom! _____

ff

Student
Book Page
24

BOATMEN STOMP

Composer: Michael A. Gray
Text: D.D. Emmett
Voicing: 3-Part Male Voices

Key: B minor/A Major
Meter: $\frac{2}{4}$
Form: Strophic
Style: Sea Chantey
Accompaniment: Piano

Programming: Concert or contest

Ranges:

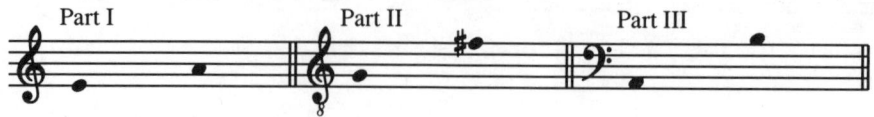

BOATMEN STOMP

Composer: Michael A. Gray
Text: D.D. Emmett
Voicing: 3-Part Male Voices

Cultural Context:

"Boatmen Stomp" was specifically written for junior high/middle school choirs with changing voices. (A "stomp" is a kind of folk dance.) The composer edited the poem, "The Boatmen Dance" and wrote music to fit the unique ranges of the boy's changing voice. "The Boatmen Dance" was first published in 1843 as an original banjo melody by D.D. Emmett who later composed "Dixie."

The oyster boat mentioned in the text is a boat that works near the shore in the shallow water. The fishing smack is a boat that can go farther out to sea. A schooner is a large boat with big sails and the steamboat's paddle-wheel leaves a wide wake in the water.

Musical Terms:

p (piano)   *mf* (mezzo forte)   *f* (forte)

‖: :‖ (repeat)   *cresc.* (crescendo)

Preparation:

Good *articulation* is essential for success with "Boatmen Stomp." To articulate means to sing or speak distinctly.

Read the following passage aloud making sure that you articulate all of the words clearly and evenly. Be especially aware of the words under the sixteenth notes. Tap the quarter note pulse as you say the words.

Hi!   Ho!   the boat-men row!   Float-in' down the riv-er on the O - hi - o!

Evaluation:

• Locate other passages in "Boatmen Stomp" that contain sixteenth notes.

• Work with a partner, chanting these lines until they are precise and clear.

Objectives:

- The student will sing with energy and clear diction. (*National Standard* 1A)
- The student will perform contemporary choral literature. (*NS* 1E)

Historical/Stylistic Guidelines:

This arrangement is an excellent example of strophic form. The energetic spirit and lively rhythms make this song a favorite for singers and audiences alike.

Michael Gray (b. 1954) was born and educated in Southern California. In addition to his work as a composer and arranger, he is a high school choral director.

Review the material found in the Cultural Context section of the student page.

Vocal Technique/Warm-Ups/Exercises:

- Articulation is the action of the lips, teeth and tip of the tongue in making sounds. (Remind the students that singing is exaggerated speech.)
- Practice the following exercise to enforce good articulation habits.

1.	Zee	zeh	zah	zoh	zee	zeh	zah	zoh	zee	zeh	zah	zoh	zoo
2.	Dee	deh	dah	doh	dee	deh	dah	doh	dee	deh	dah	doh	doo
3.	Tee	teh	tah	toh	tee	teh	tah	toh	tee	teh	tah	toh	too
4.	Hee	heh	hah	hoh	hee	heh	hah	hoh	hee	heh	hah	hoh	hoo

Repeat the exercise up by half steps.

Transpose this exercise to fit the ranges of your singers.

Rehearsal Guidelines and Notes
Suggested Sequence:

1. Familiarize students with the musical terms found in this piece as listed in the student text. (*NS* 5C)
2. Chant the words in rhythm to the first verse. Point out to the students that the three verses are very similar. Practice the rhythms to these verses .
3. When introducing the pitches to the verses, remind the singers that the parts are written in octaves.
4. Before combining the parts in the chorus, isolate and teach each part separately. Remind the students to sing with very clear articulation.
5. When rehearsing the chorus (m. 13), the rhythms should be clean and clear, especially in the sections that contain dotted eighth followed by sixteenth note patterns.
6. Isolate the last phrase (mm. 41-45) and teach as a separate lesson. This section contains long, sustained, connected notes.
7. Remind the students to make the most of the dynamics and phrase markings indicated in the score.

Performance Tips:

- Energy is the primary requirement in this piece. Sing "boisterously" as marked. Intensity, even in the soft sections is the key to a successful performance of "Boatmen Stomp."
- Take extra care when assigning voice parts in this piece. Boys with limited ranges should sing the middle part. The unchanged voices should sing the top part and divide on the cued notes.
- When singing "Boatmen Stomp," ask the students to explode the consonants and go directly to tall vowel sounds. Explode the "H" at the beginning of each chorus. ("Hi! Ho!")
- The tempo should be quick, and a speed of quarter note =100 works well for this selection.
- For variety, solos can be assigned to some of the verses.
- Some first tenors may be added to the second tenor part on the verses.
- Note that Tenor II sounds an octave lower than written.
- This arrangement can also be used for a Mixed Choir with the following voice part designations:

Soprano -	Part I
Alto -	Part I, singing cued notes where indicated
Tenor -	Part II
Bass -	Part III

Evaluation:

(From the student page)

- Locate other passages in "Boatmen Stomp" that contain sixteenth notes.

     - Work with a partner until these sections are precise and clear. (*NS* 7A, 7B)

- Listen to a recording of the choir singing "Boatmen Stomp." Do you hear the following: (*NS* 7A, 7B)

     - Clean articulation, with clear consonants and tall vowel sounds.
     - Dynamic contrast as indicated in the score.

Boatmen Stomp

For 3-Part Male Voices and Piano

The Boatmen Dance by D.D. EMMETT
By MICHAEL A. GRAY

fore the wind; The steam-boat leaves a wide_____ track o - pened:
go a-shore, They spend their cash and work_____ for more.

fore the wind; The steam-boat leaves a wide_____ track o - pened:
go a-shore, They spend their cash and work_____ for more.

Hi! Ho! the boat-men row! Float-in' down the riv - er on the

Hi! Ho! the boat-men row! Float-in' down the riv - er on the

Hi! Ho! the boat-men row! Float-in' down the riv - er on the

Student Book Page 27

O - hi - o!   Hi!   Ho!   the boat-men row! Float-in' down the riv - er on the

O - hi - o!   Hi!   Ho!   the boat-men row! Float-in' down the riv - er on the

O - hi - o!   Hi!   Ho!   the boat-men row! Float-in' down the riv - er on the

O - hi - o!

O - hi - o!

O - hi - o!

sub. **p**

Student Book Page 28

that she al-read-y was a boat-man's wife

that she al-read-y was a boat-man's wife

cresc.

Hi! Ho! the boat-men row! Float-in' down the riv - er on the O - hi - o!

Hi! Ho! the boat-men row! Float-in' down the riv - er on the O - hi - o!

Hi! Ho! the boat-men row! Float-in' down the riv - er on the O - hi - o!

Student Book Page 30

38

CHILDREN GO WHERE I SEND THEE

Composer: Traditional Spiritual,
  arranged by Emily Crocker
Text: Traditional
Voicing: TTB

Key: C minor and E♭ major
Meter: ¢
Form: Call and Response
Style: Traditional Spiritual
Accompaniment: Piano

Programming: Holiday concert or
  contest

Ranges:

Student Book Page **32**

CHILDREN GO WHERE I SEND THEE

Composer: Traditional Spiritual, arranged by Emily Crocker
Text: Traditional
Voicing: TTB

Cultural Context:
The *spiritual* is one of the first truly American forms of music. It was created by slaves who needed songs of hope during their long hours of work. Many spirituals are written in a *call and response* style. In "Children Go Where I Send Thee," one group or section calls and a larger group responds.

Emily Crocker is one of the foremost contemporary composer/arrangers in the United States. She has published well over one hundred compositions.

Musical Terms:

p (piano)	*mp* (mezzo piano)	marcato
ff (fortissimo)	*dim.* (diminuendo)	*piu mosso*
(fermata)	(accent)	*poco accel.* (poco accelerando)

Preparation:
Rhythmic precision is essential to this piece. Practice counting this exercise. Practice it once loud (forte) and once soft (piano).

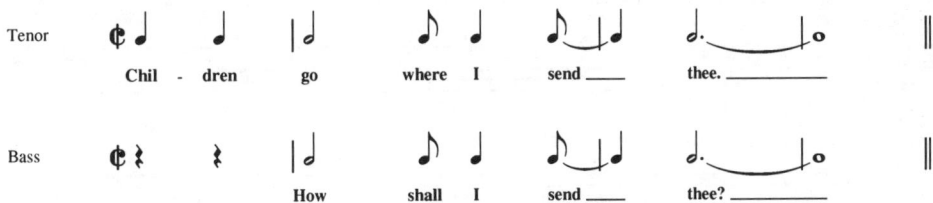

How many times can you find this pattern in your part in the first two pages of this piece?

Evaluation:
After you have learned the rhythms and pitches of this song, ask yourself these questions as you are singing:

• Are the rhythms clear and precise?

• Do you hear dynamic contrast?

Objectives:

- The student will perform rhythms with understanding and accuracy. (*National Standard* 1E)
- The student will perform dynamic and tempo changes as indicated by the composer. (*NS* 1E)
- The student will perform seasonal choral literature. (*NS* 1E)

Historical/Stylistic Guidelines:

Discuss the material found on the Cultural Context section of the student page.

"Children Go Where I Send Thee" is an arrangement of a well known spiritual. Spirituals developed in America before the Civil War when slaves turned to Biblical stories to create music of hope and relief from oppression and suffering. Spirituals have become an influential part of American culture.

Ask the students to name some spirituals. ("Swing Low, Sweet Chariot," "Didn't My Lord Deliver Daniel," "All Night, All Day," and "Precious Lord.")

"Children Go Where I Send Thee" is usually written in a major key. Emily Crocker adapted this arrangement to include both major and minor tonalities. This arrangement is a consistent favorite with choirs and audiences alike.

Vocal Technique/Warm-Ups/Exercises:

The last section of "Children Go Where I Send Thee" (mm. 52-79) contains some tricky half step intervals. Remind the singers that a half step is the smallest interval that we sing.

- Practice the following exercises and ask the students to listen carefully to the difference in the half and whole step intervals.
- Change the key as needed to fit the choir.

For more information, refer to p. 33 of *Essential Musicianship* Book I.

Rehearsal Guidelines and Notes
Suggested Sequence:

1. Familiarize students with the musical terms found in this piece as listed in the student text. (*NS* 5C)

2. Review the material found in the Preparation section of the student page.

3. Chant the words in rhythm to mm. 4-36. When the rhythms are secure, add the pitches.

4. As you are teaching the pitches, remind the students of the importance of clear articulation. Both the call and response must be articulated well for the piece to be understood.

5. Introduce the refrain section at mm. 37-46. Note the dynamic contrasts.

6. Check for understanding of the first and second ending.

7. Introduce the material in mm. 52-83 as a separate lesson. Note that this section is written in E♭ major. Be aware of the tricky half step intervals in mm. 58, 66, 70, and 78.

8. Isolate the last phrase mm. 84-90 and teach it separately.

9. Perform "Children Go Where I Send Thee" in its entirety. Identify the sections that need re-teaching.

10. Remind the students to pay close attention to the dynamics and phrase markings indicated in the music.

Performance Tips:

- Take extra care in teaching the rhythms to "Children Go Where I Send Thee." Make the students aware of the importance of good articulation. If the articulation is still not as clean as you would like, ask the students to whisper the words in rhythm. Whispering can correct careless articulation.

- Make use of the entire dynamic spectrum when teaching this piece. There are many changes and contrasts in the music that will enhance your performance.

- Unchanged voices sing the Tenor I cued notes at measure 52.

- On the last note, the music indicates going to a "hum." A resonant hum can be produced by barely putting the lips together leaving a great deal of space in the mouth. That resonance should carry throughout your performance facility.

Evaluation:
(From the Evaluation section on the student page)
After you have learned the rhythms and pitches of this song, ask yourself these questions as you are singing: (*NS* 7A, 7B)

1. Are the rhythms clear and precise?

2. Do you hear the dynamic contrast?

Extension:
Encourage the students to prepare a solo performance of a spiritual for class or concert.

Children Go Where I Send Thee

For TTB and Piano

Traditional Spiritual
Arranged by EMILY CROCKER

43

Student
Book Page
36

Student
Book Page
38

THE CRAWDAD HOLE

Composer: American Folk Song, arranged by Neil Johnson
Text: Traditional
Voicing: TBB

Key: E♭/A♭/E♭ Major
Meter: ⁴⁄₄, ¢
Form: Strophic
Style: Arranged American Folk Song

Accompaniment: Piano
Programming: Concert or festival, Americana program

Ranges:

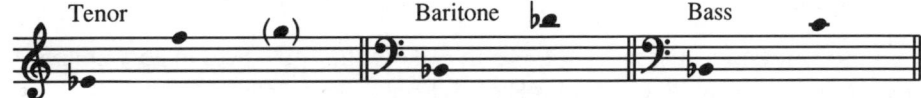

Student Book Page 40

THE CRAWDAD HOLE

Composer: American Folk Song, arranged by Neil Johnson
Text: Traditional
Voicing: TBB

Cultural Context:
American folk music takes many forms. This nonsense song probably originated in the South where crayfish (or crawdads) are plentiful. Crayfish resemble lobsters, but are much smaller in size and live in fresh water.

Musical Terms:

(♩ = 90)   (♩ = ♪)   (♩ = 90)

half time   (♩ = ♪)   *mf* (mezzo forte)

rit. (ritardando)   𝄐 (fermata)   // (caesura)

⊏⊐ (crescendo)   *f* (forte)   *mp* (mezzo piano)

⊐⊏ (decrescendo)

Preparation:
The composer has changed the style and tempo at various places in the music to add variety and humor to the song. Try singing each of these sections as described below:

• Measures 5 - 20:   Sing in a slow, blues style

• Measures 20 - 60:   Sing in a lively, energetic style

• Measures 60 - 70:   Sing in a slow, sustained style

• Measures 70 - end: Sing in a lively, energetic style

Evaluation:
• As you listen to your choir singing this song can you hear the different styles described above?

• Did you and the choir sing the song with energy and humor?

Objectives:

- The student will perform dynamic and tempo changes as indicated by the composer. (*National Standard* 1E)
- The student will sing with energy and clear diction. (*NS* 1A)

Historical/Stylistic Guidelines:

Review the material found in the Cultural Context section of the student page.

Neil Johnson was raised and educated in Minot, North Dakota, but now lives in Fort Collins, Colorado. He is currently teaching choral music at Blevins Junior High School in Fort Collins. Mr. Johnson has over thirty pieces in publication written mainly for junior high or beginning high school choirs.

Vocal Technique/Warm-Ups/Exercises:

Tuning three parts requires tall vowels, supported sound, accuracy of pitch, and good listening. Practice the exercises below to improve tuning.

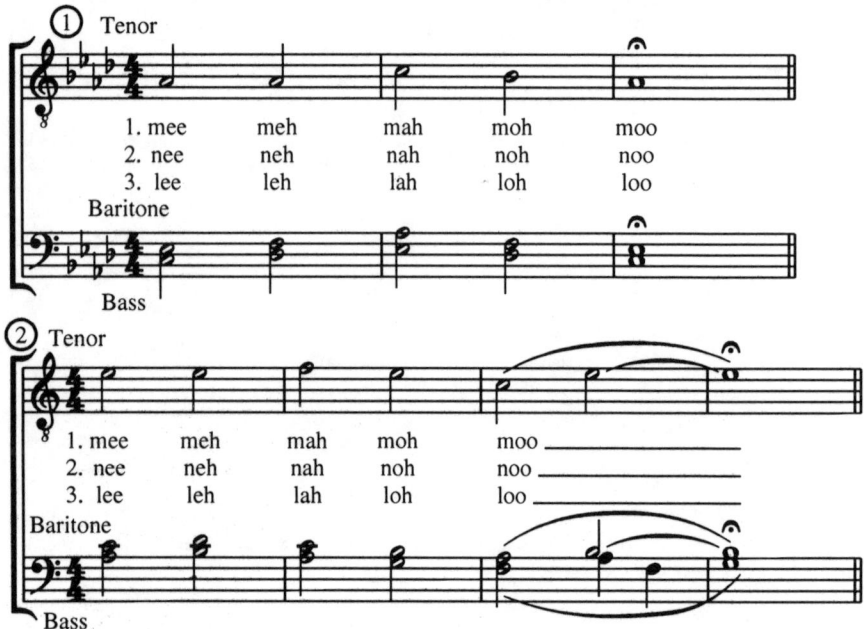

Rehearsal Guidelines and Notes
Suggested Sequence:

1. Familiarize students with the musical terms found in this piece as listed in the student text. (*NS* 5C)

2. This song is arranged in five stanzas with stylistic changes in each stanza. It is suggested that each stanza be taught separately.

   - Stanza 1 - mm. 5-20
   - Stanza 2 - mm. 24-40
   - Stanza 3 - mm. 42-57
   - Stanza 4 - mm. 60-75
   - Stanza 5 - mm. 78-97

3. Begin with stanza 1. This should be taught in a slow tempo with a "blues" feel to it. End softly with no hint of a change of tempo.

4. Teach stanza 2. It is very similar in pitches and rhythm but in strong contrast with the opening. This stanza is to be sung in a lively, energetic style at a much faster tempo.

5. Teach stanza 3 involving the key change to A♭. Check for pitch accuracy of each part. Work for blend, balance and tuning of parts.

6. In stanza 4 the tempo slows to half-time. This chorale-like section may be taught on a neutral syllable or by sight-reading. Check constantly for tuning.

7. Teach the staggered entrances on stanza 5 by having each section speak the words in rhythm measures 78-86. Cue the entrances. After the choir is very secure on the rhythm and entrances, add pitches.

8. Sing the entire song reminding students of the tempo, dynamic, and style changes required for each stanza.

Performance Tips:

- Keep the mood of this piece fun and energetic.
- Sustain the first vowel of all diphthongs. Refrain from singing the second vowel sound until the very end of the note. "Mine" is sung MAH(ee)n.
- Explode the consonants and move directly to the tall vowel sounds.
- For additional information and exercises incorporating diphthongs, refer to *Essential Musicianship* Book I, student pages 118-120.

Evaluation:

- Review and discuss the material found in the Evaluation section of the student page. (*NS* 7A, 7B)
- Create small ensembles (three to nine singers) within the group. Assign each ensemble a different verse to perform. Ask the rest of the choir to evaluate their performance. (*NS* 7A, 7B)

Extension:

Select five students to serve as team leaders to choreograph one of the five stanzas in this song. Each team leader may chose three to five students to work with him. Using outside class time, ask each group to create motions to one verse of this song. The motions should reflect the style of the stanza. After demonstrating their work to you for evaluation, have each group teach their motions to the rest of class.

The Crawdad Hole

For TBB and Piano

Traditional American Folk Song
Arranged by NEIL JOHNSON

Student Book Page 42

53

Hon - ey, ___ babe ___ of ___ mine. ___

Hon - ey, ___ babe, ___ oh babe of

Hon - ey, ___ babe, ___ oh babe of

Eb/Bb   Cm7   Fm7   Bb7   Ab

Lively (♩ = ♩) (𝅝 = 90)

mine. ___

mine. ___

Lively (♩ = ♩) (𝅝 = 90)

Eb

Student
Book Page
44

Hon - ey, __ babe of mine. __

Hon - ey, __ babe of mine. __

Hon - ey, __ babe __ of mine. __

Student Book Page 46

57

Sit-tin' on the bank 'til my feet got cold,— hon-ey.

Student
Book Page
50

61

babe ____ of mine. ____

babe ____ of mine. ____

babe ____ of mine. ____

You get a line and

Student
Book Page
52

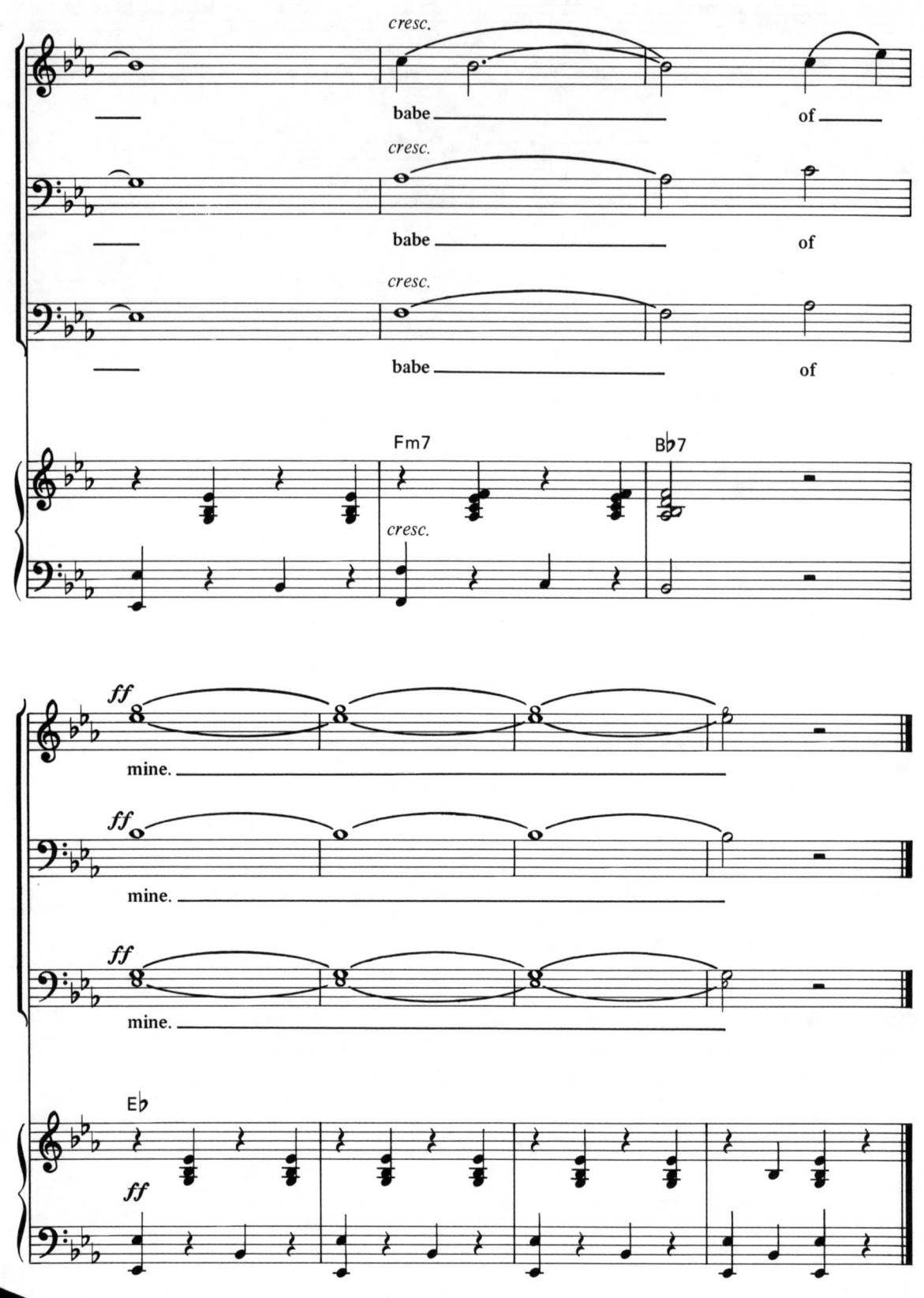

DRILL YE TARRIERS

Composer: Thomas Casey,
   arranged by Emily Crocker
Text: Thomas Casey
Voicing: TTB

Key: G minor, A minor
Meter: ¢
Form: Strophic
Style: Arranged American Folk
   Song

Accompaniment: Piano
Programming: Concert or festival,
   Americana program

Ranges:

Student Book Page 56

DRILL YE TARRIERS

Composer: Thomas Casey, arranged by Emily Crocker
Text: Thomas Casey
Voicing: TTB

Cultural Context:
During the westward expansion in American history, many American folk songs about the railroads emerged, including "Drill Ye Tarriers." Irish immigrants who came to America during the mid-1800s were given the nickname "Tarriers." They found jobs building the railroads, but were forced to work under terrible conditions. In typical "tall tale" fashion, this song tells the story of one Tarrier who was blasted in the air by a dynamite blast, then docked pay for "the time he was up in the sky."

Musical Terms:

($\downarrow$ = 96)   ◢◣ (crescendo)   ◣◢ (decrescendo)

mf (mezzo forte)   *rit.* (ritardando)   *mf* (mezzo forte)

◠ (fermata)   tempo primo $\downarrow$ (accent)

poco a poco   *decresc.* (decrescendo)   *f* (forte)

ff (fortissimo)   opt. div. (optional divisi)

Preparation:
To add excitement and energy to a song, as a singer you must pay careful attention to the dynamic markings in the music. Read the words below using the crescendos and decrescendos as marked.

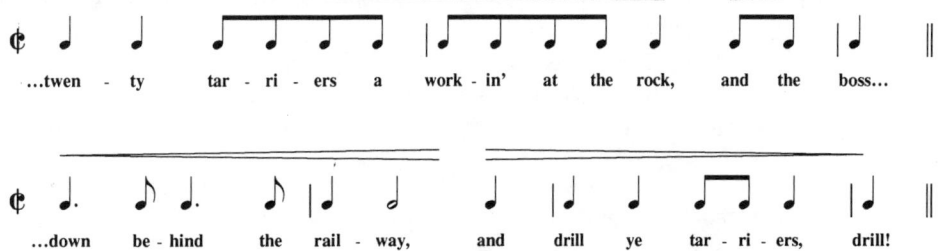

...twen - ty   tar - ri - ers   a   work - in'   at   the   rock,   and   the   boss...

...down   be - hind   the   rail - way,   and   drill   ye   tar - ri - ers,   drill!

Evaluation:
Study your music and locate the crescendos and decrescendos marked in your part. As you listen to the recording of your choir performing this piece, focus on the dynamic changes.

• Are the crescendos and decrescendos obvious to hear?

• Is there an increase in intensity on a line of repeated pitches?

(Answers to student Evaluation)
Crescendos are located in: mm. 7-8, 11-12, 15, 19-20, 28-29, 32-33, 36, 40-41, 57, 67-68. Decrescendos are located in: mm. 8-9, 21-22, 29-30, 41-42, 62-63 (poco a poco decresc.).

Objectives:

- The student will perform dynamic and tempo changes as indicated by the composer. (*National Standard* 1E)
- The student will perform choral literature of the American folk heritage. (*NS* 6B, 9A)

Historical/Stylistic Guidelines:

Review the material concerning "Drill Ye Terriers" found in the Cultural Context section of the student page with the students.

"Drill Ye Tarriers" is an energetic, entertaining piece. The rhythmic accuracy, exaggerated consonants, and dynamic contrasts are essential to the success of this piece. Your students should have great fun with it!

Emily Crocker lives and works in Milwaukee, Wisconsin. She taught public school music for fifteen years before joining the music publishing industry.

Vocal Technique/Warm-Ups/Exercises:

- Review and practice the material concerning crescendos and decrescendos found in the Preparation section of the student page.
- To prepare the singers to sing in a minor tonality, practice the following exercise. Ascend by half-steps to G and back down to F.

nee nee nee nee nee nee nee nee   noh_____   mee mee meh meh mah mah moh moh moo

Rehearsal Guidelines and Notes
Suggested Sequence:

1. Familiarize students with the musical terms found in this piece as listed in the student text. (*NS* 5C)
2. Approach the song by teaching it a cappella in verse-chorus segments. Add the piano accompaniment later.

   - verse 1/chorus at m. 5
   - verse 2/chorus at m. 26
   - verse 3/chorus at. m. 47
   - coda at m. 65

3. As you teach verses 1 and 2, the boys will soon discover that the pitches and rhythm are the same. Teach each part separately, then combine parts.
4. Verse 3 changes in key, tempo, harmony, and mood. This is an excellent spot to teach sight reading. The straight quarter note rhythm and slower tempo make it accessible to reading. The *tempo primo* chorus is the same as before.
5. Teach the coda with particular emphasis on the dynamic contrast with a gradual *decrescendo* in mm. 64-66 and a *subito forte* in m. 67.
6. Perform the entire song with piano accompaniment.

Performance Tips:

- Increase the intensity when notes are repeated on the same pitch (mm. 7-8, mm. 11-12, etc.).
- Emphasize the consonants to add energy to the singing.
- Encourage the boys to sing this song with energy and gusto (not to be confused with oversinging).
- Verse 3, with its smooth legato line, serves as a contrast to the rest of the song.

Evaluation:

- Review the material found in the Evaluation section of the student page. Discuss the many dynamic changes found in this piece. (*NS* 7A, 7B)
- Create a chart or checklist of each dynamic marking in the piece identified by measure numbers. Provide choices on the chart for: Excellent, Good, and Needs Improvement. As the choir listens to a performance tape, direct them to evaluate their dynamic levels by marking the chart or checklist. (*NS* 7A, 7B)

Extension:

Ask interested students to research information about other railroad folk songs written throughout American history. (*NS* 8B)

Drill Ye Tarriers

For TTB and Piano

Words and Music by THOMAS CASEY
Arranged by EMILY CROCKER

70

boss comes a-long and he says "keep still, and come down heav-y on the cast iron drill." And

boss comes a-long and he says "keep still, and come down heav-y on the cast iron drill." And

boss comes a-long and he says "keep still, and come down heav-y on the cast iron drill." And

drill ye tar-ri-ers, drill. Drill, oh drill! Oh, it's work all

drill ye tar-ri-ers, drill. Drill, oh drill ye tar-ri-ers, work all

drill_____ ye tar-ri-ers, drill ye tar-ri-ers drill! Oh, it's work all day for the

Student Book Page 58

day   way   down be-hind the rail-way, and drill ye tar-ri-ers, drill!

day   way   down be-hind the rail-way, and drill ye tar-ri-ers, drill!

sug-ar in your tay   down be-hind the rail-way, and drill ye tar-ri-ers, drill!

Our new fore-man is   Dan Mc-Cann,—I   tell you, sure, he's a

Our new fore-man is   Dan Mc-Cann,—I   tell you, sure, he's a

Our new fore-man is   Dan Mc-Cann,—I   tell you, sure, he's a

blame mean man! Last_ week a pre-ma-ture blast went off, and a mile in the air went

blame mean man! Last_ week a pre-ma-ture blast went off, and a mile in the air went

blame mean man! Last week a pre-ma-ture blast went off, and a mile in the air went

34

big Jim Goff. And drill ye tar-ri-ers, drill! Drill, oh drill! Oh, it's

big Jim Goff. And drill ye tar-ri-ers, drill! Drill, oh drill ye tar-ri-ers,

big Jim Goff. And drill_____ ye tar-ri-ers, drill ye tar-ri-ers, drill! Oh, it's

73

work all day way down be-hind the rail-way, and drill ye tar-ri-ers,

work all day way down be-hind the rail-way, and drill ye tar-ri-ers,

work all day for the sug-ar in your tay down be-hind the rail-way, and drill ye tar-ri-ers,

rit. **47** *mf* **A little slower, freely in four**

drill! Next time pay-day comes a-round, Jim

drill! Next time pay-day comes a-round, Jim

drill! Next time pay-day comes a-round, Jim

47 **A little slower, freely in four**

Goff was short one buck, he found, "What for?" says he, then this re-ply, "You're

Goff was short one buck, he found, "What for?" says he, then this re-ply, "You're

Goff was short one buck, he found, "What for?" says he, then this re-ply, "You're

Tempo primo   55

docked for the time you were up in the sky." And drill ye tar-ri-ers, drill. Drill, oh

docked for the time you were up in the sky." And drill ye tar-ri-ers, drill. Drill, oh

docked for the time you were up in the sky." And drill_____ ye tar-ri-ers, drill ye tar-ri-ers

75

EIGHT NIGHTS, EIGHT LIGHTS (THE STORY OF HANUKKAH)

Composer: Roger Emerson
Text: Roger Emerson

Key: F, D, G with modal influence
Meter: $\frac{3}{4}$
Form: A B A
Voicing: TBB
Style: Contemporary
    homophonic (Hanukkah)

Accompaniment: Piano
Programming: Holiday program

Ranges:

*Student
Book Page
64*

EIGHT NIGHTS, EIGHT LIGHTS (THE STORY OF HANUKKAH)

Composer: Roger Emerson
Text: Roger Emerson
Voicing: TBB

Cultural Context:
This song, set for Tenor Bass chorus, tells the story of Hanukkah. In 165 B.C., the Jews won a victory over the Syrians (Greeks) and obtained religious freedom. As they celebrated their victory in the Temple of Jerusalem they found only one small cruse of oil with which to light their holy lamps. But, miraculously, the cruse provided enough oil to keep their lamps burning for eight days and nights until new oil could be purified.

Roger Emerson, the composer of this song, is well-known for his original works and arrangements for young choirs. Formerly an instrumental and vocal music teacher, he now writes choral music full-time from his home in northern California.

Musical Terms:

mf (mezzo forte)	*molto rit.* (molto ritardando)	**D.S. al Coda**
⊕ (Coda)	𝄋 (sign)	*f* (forte)
To Coda	mysterioso	＿＿＿＿＿＿ (decrescendo)
mp (mezzo piano)	' (breath mark)	*cresc.* (crescendo)

Preparation:
This arrangement lends itself well to practicing good, tall vowels. Practice the following words, giving special attention to vowel shapes. Good vowel sounds will give your choir good tone and a maturity of sound.

night = nah(ee)t   of = ahv   celebration= cel-eh-brae-shahn

light = lah(ee)t   us = ahs   the = thah

dedication = ded-ih-kae-shahn

Evaluation:
Give each member of your choir a number.

• Let the even numbered choir members sing the opening phrase (mm. 9-16) and let the odd numbered choir members listen for tall vowels.

• Reverse tasks.

Objectives:

- The student will sing with tall, uniform vowels. (*National Standard* 1A)
- The student will perform holiday choral literature. (*NS* 1E)

Historical/Stylistic Guidelines:

Hanukkah (HAN-nu-kah) is the Jewish festival of lights or Feast of Dedication. The Hebrew word for Hanukkah (also written Hanukkah) can be divided into two words: Chanu which means rested: and Kah which indicates the Hebrew number 25. The Jews rested on the 25th day of Kislev (December) from their battles with the Greeks. The Hanukkah holiday begins on the eve of the 25th day of Kislev and lasts for eight days.

During Hanukkah, gifts are exchanged and contributions are made to the poor. Each evening, one candle is lit in a special eight branched candelabrum called a Menorah. One candle is added every night until the total reaches eight on the last night.

The history of Hanukkah begins in 165 B.C. when the Jews, after a three year struggle, defeated the Greek Syrian King, Antiochus. They held festivities in the temple in Jerusalem, and dedicated it to God. According to the Talmud, when the Jews cleaned the temple, they found only one small cruse of oil with which to light their holy lamps. But, miraculously, the cruse provided them oil for eight days until the new oil could be purified. Other sources tell of a torchlight parade in the temple which may also have contributed to the tradition of lighting candles on Hanukkah.

Roger Emerson is one of the most widely performed choral composers in America today. Mr. Emerson is a consistent winner of the ASCAP Standard Award, and was honored by the performance of his arrangement of "America" at the Kennedy Center during the ceremonies inaugurating President George Bush. Mr. Emerson taught for several years, but now devotes all of his time to composing and consulting at his home in Mt. Shasta, California.

Vocal Technique/Warm-Ups/Exercises:

- "Eight Nights, Eight Lights" is full of long phrases that require excellent tone, good breath support and the ability to sing musical phrases.
- Sing the following exercise, remembering the following:

  1. In $\frac{3}{4}$ time, beat one is the stressed beat, and beats two and three are secondary beats.
  2. Sing four-bar phrases instead of two-bar phrases.
  3. Keep the vowel sounds very tall in the underlined words.

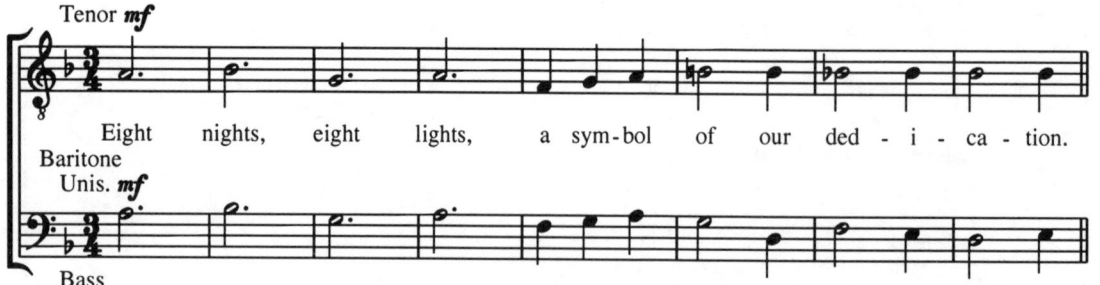

Rehearsal Guidelines and Notes:
Suggested Sequence:

1. Familiarize students with the musical terms found in this piece as listed in the student text. (*NS 5C*)

2. Review the material found in the Cultural Context section of the student page with the students.

3. Introduce the theme found in mm. 9-16 (it returns at mm. 63-70). Pay particular attention to the half step intervals found in m. 14 and m. 15. Remind the students that a half step is the smallest interval that we sing.

4. Introduce the 3-part call and response refrain found at mm. 17-26. Point out that this refrain returns at mm. 71-79. Remind the students that the baritone part has the melody throughout the chorus. Ask the first tenors and basses to stress the first beat of each response.

5. When introducing the material at m. 29, the tone should be legato. Again, take some extra rehearsal time with the half step intervals.

6. Isolate the last three measures (mm. 80-82), and teach them as a separate lesson. The rhythmic pattern and the vocal lines are quite different in this section. There may be a need to reassign some of the voice parts in this section due to the ranges.

7. Check for understanding with regard to the terms D.S. al Coda and Coda.

8. Perform "Eight Nights, Eight Lights" in its entirety. Identify the sections that need re-teaching.

9. Remind the singers to make the most of the dynamic markings in the score.

Performance Tips:

- The text is paramount in this selection. Check for proper diction and articulation throughout.

- If some of the unison passages are out of range for the singers, ask the singers to drop out until the range is more comfortable.

- When teaching this piece, ask the students to sing in four-bar phrases rather than three-bar phrases.

- The introduction may be repeated softly while portions of the historical guidelines are narrated to the audience.

Evaluation:

Give each member of your choir a number.

1. Let the even-numbered choir members sing the opening phrase (mm. 9-16) and let the odd-numbered choir members listen for tall vowels.

2. Reverse tasks. (*NS 7A, 7B*)

Extension:

- Encourage the students to prepare a solo performance of a holiday song for class or concert.

- Encourage students to create a composition in ABA form using "Eight Nights, Eight Lights" as a model. (*NS 4A*)

Eight Nights, Eight Lights
(The Story Of Hanukkah)

For TBB and Piano

Words and Music by
ROGER EMERSON

Student Book Page 65

a sym - bol of our ded - i - ca - tion.

Eight ___ nights ___ eight ___ lights, ___

Eight nights, eight lights,

Eight ___ nights, ___ eight ___ lights ___

To Coda

join us in joy - ous cel - e - bra -

Unis.

Student Book Page 66

81

82

Student
Book Page
68

The lamps kept on burn - ing for eight days and

nights, giv - ing us rea - son to

cel - e - brate! Cel - e - brate! Cel - e - brate!

D.S. al Coda

84

I WILL SING HALLELUJAH

Composer: Neil A. Johnson
Key: F Major
Text: Neil A. Johnson
Voicing: TTB

Meter: ¢
Form: A B A B A coda
Style: Contemporary spiritual
Accompaniment: Piano

Programming: Concert or festival; opportunity for solo singing

Ranges:

I WILL SING HALLELUJAH

Composer: Neil A. Johnson
Text: Neil A. Johnson
Voicing: TTB

Student Book Page 72

Cultural Context:

This contemporary song is written in the style of a *spiritual*. To create this style, the composer used two techniques: *syncopation* and *call and response*. Syncopation is the stressing of notes on the "off beats." In call and response, a soloist sings a line or phrase answered by a group of singers. In this song, the basses sing alone (call) and all voices answer (response), then the tenors sing alone (call) and all voices answer (response).

Musical Terms:

f (forte)   *mp* (mezzo forte)   *mf* (mezzo forte)

cued notes   (slide)   (crescendo)

no rit. (no ritardando)   syncopation   call and response

Preparation:

Practice these syncopated rhythms found in the music:

1.

2.

3.

With a pencil, circle each syncopated rhythm you find in your music.

Evaluation:

Listen to an audio recording of your class performing this song. As you listen, follow along in your music to check for the following:

- Did the choir sing the syncopated rhythms accurately and together?
- Did the choir put the stress on the "off beats" when singing?
- Was there a contrast between the call and response sections?

If you can answer "yes" to the questions above, then you are well on your way to singing in a spiritual style.

Objectives:

- The student will perform syncopated rhythms with understanding and accuracy. (*National Standard* 1E)
- The student will develop an understanding of the American spiritual through discussion and performance. (*NS 6B, 6C, 9A*)

Historical/Stylistic Guidelines:

Neil Johnson was raised and educated in Minot, North Dakota, but now lives in Fort Collins, Colorado. He is currently teaching choral music at Blevins Junior High School in Fort Collins. Mr. Johnson has over thirty pieces in publication written mainly for junior high or beginning high school choirs.

"I Will Sing Hallelujah" is a contemporary spiritual, a piece written in the style of a spiritual, rather than an arrangement of a pre-existing spiritual. It is to be sung with energy and with the stressing of syncopated rhythms.

Vocal Technique/Warm-Ups/Exercises:

Practice these chord progressions slowly, first on "loo" then on "hallelu," listening carefully for correct tuning. This will help prepare the singers for the 3-part harmony in the response sections of the two verses.

Rehearsal Guidelines and Notes
Suggested Sequence:

1. Familiarize students with the musical terms found in this piece as listed in the student text. (*NS 5C*)

2. This song is repetitive, making it easier to learn, but it contains some tricky rhythms and close 3-part harmony, making it more challenging than it appears.

3. Start with verse 1(mm. 23-37) and verse 2 (mm. 56-70). The pitches and rhythms are the same. Teach each part by rote or by having the singers sight-read their part. Explain that this is the call and response section described in the Cultural Context on the student page.

4. When combining the parts it may be necessary to isolate the "hallelu's" to correct tuning. Refer to the Vocal Technique exercise in this lesson for further practice.

5. Shift focus to the chorus as it appears at the beginning (mm. 6-21).

   - Direct the singers to chant the words in rhythm. Check for accuracy.
   - Add pitches, one voice part at a time, by rote or sight reading.
   - Combine the parts.

88

6. Repeat this process for the chorus as repeated two more times (mm. 39-54 and mm. 72-end). (They are exactly the same, except for the six measure coda at the end.) Spend time practicing the coda.

7. Sing the entire song paying close attention to the dynamics as indicated in the score.

Performance Tips:

• The Tenor I and Tenor II will probably need to sing the cued notes at the beginning of the chorus each time.

• Experiment with different students singing a solo at the call sections of the verses.

• Because of the repetition, exaggerate the dynamic levels to create variety in the performance. Sing the first phrase of chorus loudly, then the second phrase softly as an echo. Also, try making a large dynamic contrast between the solo and the response.

Evaluation:

Review the material found in the Evaluation section on the student page. (*NS 7A, 7B*) Lead students as they answer the questions.

Extension:

• Ask students to compare and contrast "I Will Sing Hallelujah" with other spirituals found in this book: "Children Go Where I Send Thee," "Mary Had a Baby," and "This Train."

• Encourage students to create a rhythmic improvisation using syncopated rhythmic patterns from "I Will Sing Hallelujah." Use clapping and/or classroom instruments. (*NS 3C*)

I Will Sing Hallelujah

For TTB and Piano

Words and Music by
NEIL A. JOHNSON

Student Book Page 73

Student Book Page 76

94

Student
Book Page
80

earned his crown, ___ Hal - le, Hal - le - lu. ___ So I'll sing hal - le - lu -

earned his crown, ___ Hal - le, Hal - le - lu. ___ So I'll sing hal - le - lu -

Hal - le, Hal - le - lu. ___ So I'll sing hal - le - lu -

Bb7   F   72 F

- jah, ___ And you'll sing hal - le - lu, ___ We'll go march - ing

- jah, ___ And you'll sing hal - le - lu, ___ We'll go march - ing

- jah, ___ And you'll sing hal - le - lu, ___ We'll go march - ing

F7/G   Bb   F   Fmaj7/G F7/G Bb

Student Book Page 81

*If possible, 1st and 2nd tenor should sing divisi the top staff, baritone sing the middle staff and bass sing the bottom staff.

Student Book Page 82

hal - le - lu - jah, Come sing hal - le - lu.

hal - le - lu - jah, Come sing hal - le - lu.

hal - le - lu - jah, Come sing hal - le - lu.

F   Dm   Gm7   Gm/C   F

no rit.

no rit.

no rit.

B♭   Bdim7   F/C   F   G♯dim7   Em   F

no rit.

IT'S THE CHRISTMAS TIME OF YEAR

Composer: Jack Kunz
Text: Jack Kunz
Voicing: TBB

Key: G major
Meter: $\frac{4}{4}$
Form: A A B A
Style: Contemporary, secular, holiday

Accompaniment: Piano with optional bells or chimes
Programming: Seasonal concert; excellent for beginning choirs

Ranges:

Tenor   Baritone   Bass

Student Book Page **84**

IT'S THE CHRISTMAS TIME OF YEAR

Composer: Jack Kunz
Text: Jack Kunz
Voicing: TBB

Cultural Context:
This secular holiday selection for Tenor Bass Chorus uses the voice to imitate the sound of holiday bells or chimes.

Musical Terms:

$\overset{>}{\cdot}$ (accent) f (forte) $f\!f$ (fortissimo)

$m\!f$ (mezzo forte)   *slight ritard.* (ritardando) $\frown$ (fermata)

Preparation:
The dotted eighth note followed by a sixteenth note is used throughout "It's the Christmas Time of Year." Speak the following passage in rhythm. Be sure to "bounce" off the sixteenth notes, but be careful that you don't close to the "n" on the word "in" and "ng" on the word "ring."

Bring in the sea-son with the play-ing of the chimes. Bring in the sea-son with the play-ing of the chimes.

Ring them loud and clear, ring them far and near, it's the Christ-mas time of year.

Evaluation:
Rehearse the "bell" section of this song (mm. 19-30). As a general rule, singers always sing "on the vowel." For the special effect needed, close to the "ng" of "ring" to achieve a "bell-like" sound to your voice.

Do you know the English literature term that describes words which are formed by a vocal imitation of the sound associated with the meaning of the word? Can you think of other words that are examples of this particular term?

(Answer to Evaluation question)
Onomatopoeia is the term.
Other examples are *buzz* and *hiss*.

Objectives:

- The student will sing with energy and clear diction. (*National Standard* 1A)
- The student will perform rhythms with understanding and accuracy. (*NS* 1E)
- The student will perform seasonal choral literature. (*NS* 1E)

Historical/Stylistic Guidelines:

Throughout the ages, the use of bells in music has been very popular. In 8th century China, bells were used to represent the high musical culture of the day. Bells were used as percussion instruments for both festive and solemn occasions during the 14th and 15th centuries, and bells have been part of religious services since the 6th century. Bells dating back to 100 B.C. have been discovered in Egypt and China. Today, bells come in all shapes and sizes from weights of less than an ounce to well over one hundred tons.

There are two ways to strike a bell:

- chiming - the hammer (or clapper) is moved to strike the side of the bell.
- ringing - the bell is moved around in a complete circle.

Chimes consist of a set of tubes of various lengths suspended from a frame and struck with mallets (or a hammer). Chimes are often used to simulate church bells because they have a broad dynamic range and accurate pitch.

If possible, try to find chimes or handbells to enhance your performance of "It's the Christmas Time of Year."

Vocal Technique/Warm-Ups/Exercises:

- Much of the harmony found in "It's the Christmas Time of Year" is written in thirds.
- Practice the following exercise as an ear training drill.

Rehearsal Guidelines and Notes
Suggested Sequence:

1. Familiarize students with the musical terms found in this piece as listed in the student text. (*NS* 5C)
2. Review the material found in the Preparation section of the student page.
3. Chant the rhythms to mm. 1-17. Point out that mm. 1-8 and 9-17 are identical sections.
4. Add the pitches to this section as a sight-singing exercise.
5. Introduce the middle section (mm. 19-30). Check that students understand the accent marks.
6. Teach the last section (mm. 37-46). Remind the singers that this section is like the first two sections of the piece. Place some of the unchanged boys' voices on the optional Tenor I G at the end.
7. Remind the students to pay particular attention to the dynamic markings indicated in the score.

102

Performance Tips:

- This piece is scored for 3-part male voices (TBB), with Part I in the treble clef and Parts II and III in the bass clef. It may also be performed with the two top voices scored in the treble clef (SAB).
- This piece may be transposed up a perfect 4th for younger men's voices.
- Mm. 33-36 may be eliminated if chimes are unavailable.
- In mm. 21-30, place a strong accented emphasis on the word "ring" and sustain the "ng" sound.
- If necessary, have the accompanist play measures 7 and 8 as an introduction.
- Remind the students to sustain the notes for their full value, especially when there is a suspension in the bass part (mm. 8, 16).
- At m. 37, be aware that this section should be taken slower and should be sung "triumphantly."
- Remind the students to sing with clear diction and crisp articulation.

Evaluation:

Listen to a recording of the choir singing "It's the Christmas Time of Year." Listen for the following: (*NS 7A, 7B*)

- Clear rhythmic passages
- Crisp clear diction
- The word "ring" sounding like a bell

Extension:

What other holiday songs can you name that use or mention bells? (Some examples are: "Jingle Bells," "Silver Bells," "Ding Dong! Merrily on High!," and "Carol of the Bells.")

It's The Christmas Time Of Year

For TBB and Piano with Optional Chimes

Performance Suggestions:

1. This piece is scored for 3-Part male voices (TBB), with Part I in treble clef and Parts II and III in the bass clef.
2. This piece may also be transposed up a perfect 4th for younger men's voices.
3. Measure 33-36 may be eliminated if chimes are unavailable.
4. In measures 21-30, place a strong accented emphasis on the word "ring" and sustain the "ng" sound.

Words and Music by
JACK KUNZ

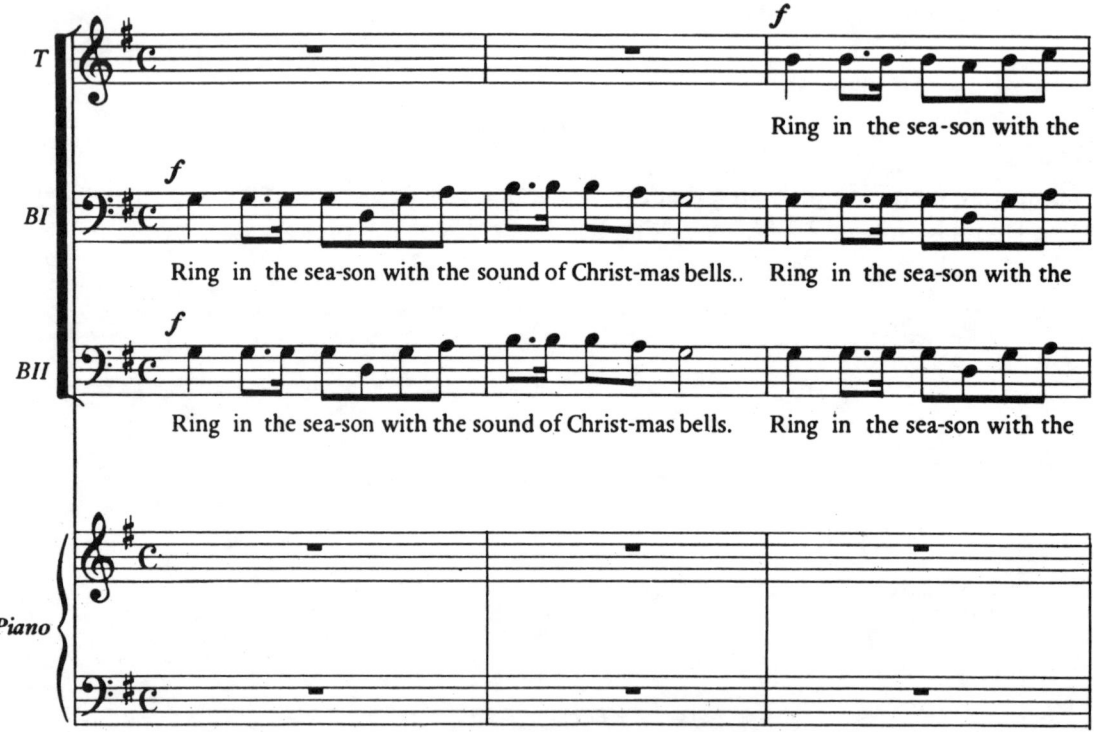

Ring in the sea-son with the
Ring in the sea-son with the sound of Christ-mas bells.. Ring in the sea-son with the
Ring in the sea-son with the sound of Christ-mas bells. Ring in the sea-son with the

Student Book Page 85

sound of Christ-mas bells.   Ring them loud and clear,   ring them far and near,

sound of Christ-mas bells.   Ring them loud and clear,   ring them far and near,

sound of Christ-mas bells.   Ring them loud and clear,   ring them far and near,

mf

it's the Christ-mas time of   year.

it's the Christ-mas time of   year.   Bring   in   the sea-son with the

it's the Christ-mas time of   year._____   Bring   in   the sea-son with the

Bring in the sea-son with the play-ing of the chimes.

play-ing of the chimes. Bring in the sea-son with the play-ing of the chimes.

play-ing of the chimes. Bring in the sea-son with the play-ing of the chimes.

Ring them loud and clear, ring them far and near, it's the Christ-mas time of

Ring them loud and clear, ring them far and near, it's the Christ-mas time of

Ring them loud and clear, ring them far and near, it's the Christ-mas time of

year, it's here!

year, it's here!

year,_____ it's here!

Ring out the

Ring the bells for

bells, ring, ring, ring! Ring out the

Student
Book Page
88

Student
Book Page
89

109

play-ing of the chimes. Ring them loud and clear, ring them far and near,

play-ing of the chimes. Ring them loud and clear, ring them far and near,

play-ing of the chimes. Ring them loud and clear, ring them far and near,

it's the Christ-mas time of year, it's here!_____

it's the Christ-mas time of year, it's here!_____

it's the Christ-mas time of year, it's here!_____

MARY HAD A BABY

Composer: Traditional Christmas Spiritual, arranged by Roger Emerson

Text: Traditional

Voicing: TBB

Key: A Major/F# Major

Meter: 4/4

Form: Strophic

Style: Contemporary spiritual written in pop style

Accompaniment: Piano with guitar chords included

Programming: Concert, seasonal performance

Ranges:

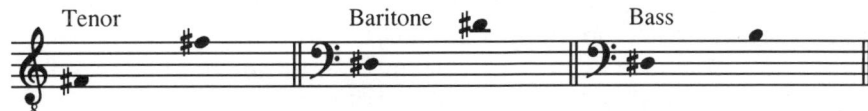

Student Book Page **92**

MARY HAD A BABY

Composer: Traditional Christmas Spiritual, arranged by Roger Emerson

Text: Traditional

Voicing: TBB

Cultural Context:

"Mary Had a Baby" is a traditional *spiritual* which appears in many versions and arrangements. In this arrangement, Roger Emerson makes use of spoken words as well as singing. In addition, he has made each verse unique by writing slightly different harmonies.

Musical Terms:

˟ (spoken)	*mp* (mezzo piano)	*cresc.* (crescendo)
mf (mezzo forte)	*dim.* (diminuendo)	*molto rit.* (molto ritardando)
sub. (subito)	*div.* (divisi)	(fermata)

Preparation:

Use these exercises to help you practice holding your part securely while the other parts sing something different.

Things to notice:

1. Did you hold your notes full value?

2. Did you hold a steady pitch even though other parts changed?

3. Could you hold the notes full value with a light, unforced tone quality?

4. In your music, circle all the places where your part holds a note while other parts change.

Evaluation:

After you have learned the rhythms and pitches of "Mary Had a Baby," check how well you can stay on pitch while other parts move. Divide into trios (tenor, baritone, and bass) and sing mm. 17-20. Listen to the small groups. Use the following statements to describe each performance:

1. Great. Each singer held a steady pitch, held notes for full value, and had a good light tone quality.

2. Good. Each singer held a steady pitch most of the time and held most notes full value.

3. Good try, but singers sang out of tune and did not hold notes for full value.

Note: You may want to do this several times with different combinations of singers as you learn the song more completely.

(Answers to question 4 in Preparation)
mm. 5-6, 7-8, 17-18, 19-20, 27-28, 29-30, 37-38, and 39-40.

Objectives:

- The student will perform dynamic and tempo changes as indicated by the composer. (*National Standard* 1E)
- The student will perform seasonal choral literature. (*NS* 1E)

Historical/Stylistic Guidelines:

David Ewen remarks in *All the Years of American Popular Music* (p. 32), that "unlike many other American folk songs, the spiritual was created not by an individual, but by groups; it was meant to be sung chorally, not solo. Consequently — almost unique in American folk music — the interest lies not only in the melody but in the harmony." "Mary Had a Baby" is an example of a spiritual in which harmony is especially important because it is a "call and response" designed to be sung by a soloist and answered by a group of singers.

Roger Emerson is one of the most widely performed choral composers and arrangers in America today, with over 375 titles in print, and nine million copies in circulation. He received his degree in choral music education from Southern Oregon State College and taught for seven years in the Mt. Shasta Public School System. He concluded his teaching career by conducting the vocal jazz program at the College of the Siskiyous, and now resides in Mt. Shasta, California. Other Emerson works in this volume include: "Eight Nights, Eight Lights" and "This Train."

Vocal Technique/Warm-Ups/Exercises:

- Rehearse the Preparation section of the student page to prepare singers for the harmony in "Mary Had a Baby."
- Avoid possible intonation problems using the following exercise:

    - This exercise is based on mm. 10-13 and appears throughout the song. It isolates the pitches from the rhythm of the song and lets the singers concentrate on the harmony.
    - Hold each chord until it tunes.
    - Encourage students to sing the third of the chord and the seventh degree of the scale high.

Rehearsal Guidelines and Notes
Suggested Sequence:

1. Familiarize students with the musical terms found in this piece as listed in the student text. (*NS* 5C)
2. Learn the first verse (mm. 5-13) by chanting the rhythm and then learning the pitch. Learn the three-part section (mm. 10-13) by using exercises in the Vocal Techniques section of the teacher's edition and the Preparation section of the student page.
3. Point out how the verse follows a call ("Mary had a baby") and response ("yes Lord") pattern.
4. Sing verse 2 (m. 17) and verse 3 (m. 27), pointing out the small differences in the parts.
5. Before teaching the fourth verse (mm. 37-end), discuss the way the arranger has changed this verse (Basses and Baritones have the call and the Tenors have the response).
6. Finally, as all parts are rehearsed together, remind the singers to pay particular attention to the dynamic markings indicated in the score.
7. Add accompaniment after all parts are secure.

Performance Tips:

- Hold all notes full value.

- Make an exercise similar to the one in the Vocal Technique section of the teacher's edition which isolates pitches from rhythm to rehearse the harmonies on the last page.

- Remind singers to avoid oversinging by performing the *piano* sections softer rather than singing the *forte* sections louder. This is a good vehicle to make each individual singer aware of how much dynamic contrast his own voice can control. Remind boys with changing voices that their voices will become more consistent and more powerful as their voice change progresses.

- Remind singers to make each phrase different and to sing phrases, not just notes.

- Consider using contrasting dynamics and judicious use of rubato to create a musical performance.

Evaluation:

- Assess student progress at maintaining a steady pitch by completing the Evaluation section of the student page. (*NS 7A, 7B*)

- Record a rehearsal performance and ask singers to analyze where dynamic contrasts could have been greater. Can the chorus sing *forte* or *fortissimo* and still keep a rich, in-tune sound? (*NS 7A, 7B*)

Extension:

If possible, have students listen to other male groups singing with a great deal of dynamic contrast. The very best models may come from boys who attend high school in your area. If a recording of a good high school male group is not available, try listening to commercial recordings by The King's Singers (a male choral group from England) or The Vocal Majority (a male barbershop chorus from Dallas).

Mary Had A Baby

For TBB and Piano

Traditional Christmas Spiritual
Adapted and Arranged by ROGER EMERSON

Student Book Page 93

Student Book Page 95

118

PASSING BY

Composer: Emily Crocker
Text: Robert Herrick
Voicing: TTB

Key: B♭ Major
Meter: 4/4
Form: Strophic
Style: Lyric contemporary
Accompaniment: Piano; may be performed a cappella

Programming: Contest or festival, concert; good piece to teach expressive phrasing

Ranges:

Student Book Page **98**

PASSING BY

Composer: Emily Crocker
Text: Robert Herrick
Voicing: TTB

Cultural Context:

This famous text by noted 17th century English poet, Robert Herrick, tells the story of a man who falls in love with someone he sees from a distance ("I did but see her passing by."), and goes on to describe why she is so wonderful ("was never face so pleased my mind."). Many famous composers have written songs to this text. In this version, composer Emily Crocker has written a completely new melody for these famous words.

Musical Terms:

rubato	(♩ = ca. 84)	*mf* (mezzo forte)
mp (mezzo piano)	———————— (crescendo)	———————— (decrescendo)
⌐¹——————— (1st ending)	⌐²——————— (2nd ending)	*f* (forte)
rit. (ritardando)	‖: :‖ (repeat signs)	unis. (unison)
' (breath mark)	⌢ (fermata)	

Preparation:

One of the challenges of this piece is to control your voice so that you can get gradually louder and softer and still keep a light, controlled tone quality. Practice these exercises on a neutral syllable.

Sing this exercise by starting very softly, adding a crescendo and decrescendo in the middle, and ending very softly. Most people do not have that much control. Sing the crescendos and decrescendos with a clear light tone and without going off pitch.

Evaluation:

After you have learned this song, add dynamics to each phrase. For example, can you add controlled crescendos and decrescendos to "There is a lady sweet and kind"?

119

Objectives:

- The student will develop the posture and breath control adequate for supporting sustained phrases. (*National Standard* 1A)
- The student will listen critically as a participating member of an ensemble, concentrating on the balance of the voice parts. (*NS* 7A, 7B)
- The student will demonstrate the ability to blend with other ensemble voices utilizing appropriate tone quality, diction, and intonation. (*NS* 1E)

Historical/Stylistic Guidelines:

Emily Crocker, a native Texan, was a professional educator for fifteen years. She taught all levels of choral music, specializing in middle school/junior high, where her choirs received numerous superior ratings in concert and sight-reading competitions. In 1989, she joined the music publishing industry and is now Director of Choral Publications for Hal Leonard Corporation, Milwaukee, Wisconsin. She holds degrees from the University of North Texas and Texas Woman's University, and has done additional post-graduate work at the University of North Texas where she was assistant conductor of the A Cappella Choir and taught elementary music education classes.

Emily is known nationally as one of the premier choral writers specializing in music for young choirs. She has over 100 works currently in print, and since 1986 has been awarded ASCAP special awards for educational and concert music. Her works can be found on contest lists throughout the United States and each year she receives invitations to write commissioned works.

Vocal Technique/Warm-Ups/Exercises:

- To prepare for the vocal control needed for "Passing By," rehearse the Preparation section of the student page.
- Further emphasize dynamic control by using the harmonic exercise below (based on the last five measures of the song):

  - Sing on a neutral syllable, holding each chord until it tunes.
  - When the choir can sing the chords in tune, add as much dynamic contrast as they can effectively control.

Rehearsal Guidelines and Notes
Suggested Sequence:

1. Familiarize students with the musical terms found in this piece as listed in the student text. (*NS* 5C)
2. Learn one verse at a time following this procedure:

   - Chant the rhythm of each part. The Second Tenors may need assistance in finding their part; check for understanding and notate their part separately if needed.
   - Chant the rhythm of all three parts using words.
   - Add diction hints as they are chanting the words; use all tall vowels; enunciate beginning and ending consonants clearly; remind them to sing diphthongs correctly.

face = FEH(ee)s not fehEEs

mind = MAH(ee)nd not mahEEnd

die = DAH(ee) not dahEE

3. Learn pitches either by rote or by sight-reading; learn each line separately, then combine. The harmonic exercise in the Vocal Technique section of the teacher's edition may be helpful in learning the final verse.

4. Add the words after the pitches are secure.

5. Most importantly, remind the singers to pay particular attention to the dynamics, phrase markings, and *rubato* indicated in the score. These are absolutely essential for an expressive performance of this beautiful song.

Performance Tips:

- Stress uniformity of vowels with the enunciation of the word "passing" by asking students to sing a short "a" with an "ah" mouth shape.
- Consider singing "Passing By" a cappella. It works well with or without accompaniment.
- Work on crescendo and decrescendo within each phrase, reminding students not to sing louder than they can control.
- Breathing is clearly marked by rests in the first two verses; in the third verse, experiment with the opening phrase ("Cupid is winged and doth range her country so my love doth change."). Consider singing it as one phrase, using staggered breathing as needed.
- Increase intensity across each held or dotted note. Such remarks as "pull the phrase," "grow across the held notes," and "move" may verbally express what the music does in such spots.
- As expressively as possible, read the words aloud to the chorus and discuss the meaning with them.
- The final verse may need some interpretation. Perhaps you might use an explanation such as: Cupid, the ancient bringer of love, flies across the countryside causing people to fall in and out of love. Yet regardless of what Cupid does, even if he changes the earth or sky, the singer will love his lady until he dies.

Evaluation:

- Encourage the singers to listen to each other by completing the Evaluation section of the student page. (NS 7A, 7B)
- Listen to recordings of other choirs, asking singers to rate which ones were most effective in their use of dynamics. Try to play both good and bad examples of expressive choral singing if the recordings are available. Recordings made at festival or contest are a possible source of models for developing choirs. (NS 7A, 7B)

Extension:

"Passing By" by Edwin Purcell is a popular solo for male vocalists. It appears in the *Pathways of Song* by Frank Laforge and Will Earhart and is on many contest lists. Suggest that one of the singers perform this solo for the class, allowing a comparison of the Crocker and Purcell melodies.

Passing By

For TTB and Piano

This piece should be sung very expressively. Give attention to phrasing and dynamics, and use rubato freely. Meas. 21-22 are optional for the baritones if range is a problem.

Text by ROBERT HERRICK

Music by EMILY CROCKER

Student Book Page 99

pass - ing by, and yet I'll love her till I die.
know not why, and yet I'll love her till I die.

pass - ing by, and yet I'll love her till I die.
know not why, and yet I'll love her till I die.

17 *mf*

Cu-pid is wing - ed and doth range _____

Is wing-ed and doth range,

PIPING TIM OF GALWAY

Composer: Irish Folk Song, arranged by Frederick Swanson

Text: Traditional

Voicing: TB

Key: D Major/G Major

Meter: $\frac{4}{4}$

Form: A B A with coda

Style: Arranged Irish Folk Song

Accompaniment: Piano

Programming: Concert, contest, or festival

Ranges:

Student Book Page **102**

PIPING TIM OF GALWAY

Composer: Irish Folk Song, arranged by Frederick Swanson

Text: Traditional

Voicing: TB

Cultural Context:

Galway is a city located in the western part of Ireland where Galway Bay empties into the Atlantic Ocean.

The character in this poem is similar to that of an Irish pipe player. The wooden instrument used in this time period is similar to the flute of today. Pipes were an integral part of military and regal ceremonies in Ireland.

Musical Terms:

𝄋 (sign)   D. S. al ⊕ (D.S. al coda)   ⊕ (Coda)

⌒ (slur)

Preparation:

The tempo marking for this song is "fast and light." Look at the sixteenth note passages printed below. The sixteenth notes must be sung evenly. Make every effort to articulate these passages cleanly.

• Sing the passage four times, each time stressing the indicated sixteenth note.

• Finally, sing the passage again, stressing each sixteenth note evenly.

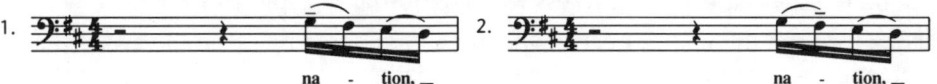

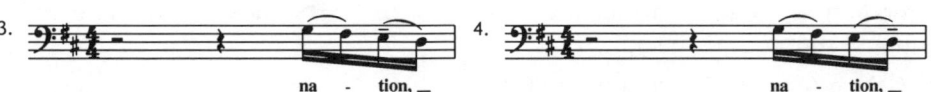

Evaluation:

Circle other sixteenth note passages in your music. Are you stressing each sixteenth note evenly and without slurring? Listen to the other sections in your choir and evaluate their progress.

Objectives:
- The student will sing with energy and clear diction. (*National Standard* 1A)
- The student will perform 16th note rhythms with understanding and accuracy. (*NS* 1E)

Historical/Stylistic Guidelines:
Review the material found in the Cultural Context section of the student page.

"Piping Tim of Galway" is an arrangement of an Irish folk song. It is similar to many 15th and 16th century secular songs that were popular in the British Isles. Along with the harp, the flute is considered a native instrument of Ireland. "Piping Tim of Galway" was probably performed on a wooden or metal "end blown" flute, rather than the transverse flute used today. Melodies such as "Piping Tim of Galway" were written with easy step-wise motion to accommodate the difficulty in playing the pipe.

Vocal Technique/Warm-Ups/Exercises:
- Review the material found in the Preparation section on the student page.
- Articulation is the action of the lips, teeth, and tip of the tongue in making sounds. Practice the following exercises to stress the importance of good articulation. Each note should be heard clearly and distinctly.

Lips, teeth, tip of the tongue; lips, teeth, tip of the tongue; lips, teeth, tip of the tongue.

Rehearsal Guidelines and Notes
Suggested Sequence:
1. Familiarize students with the musical terms found in this piece as listed in the student text. (*NS* 5C)
2. Chant the words in rhythm (mm. 2-18).
3. Learn the pitches (mm. 2-18). This piece works well as a tool to sharpen sight-reading skills.
4. Check for understanding with regard to the coda.
5. Learn the coda section (mm. 19-21) as a separate lesson. The rhythmic and melodic patterns change here. Put some of the unchanged voices on the F-sharps on the last two notes.
6. Remind the students to pay particular attention to their articulation when rehearsing "Piping Tim of Galway."

Performance Tips:
- Good energy is the key to success when performing "Piping Tim of Galway."
- Look through the text to decide where breaths should be taken. Be aware that some singers may want to clip the ends of the phrases in order to get a breath.
- Remind the students to be aware of which voice part has the melody (in m. 2-9 the bass part has the melody, and in mm. 11-18 the melody is in the tenor part). The melody should be emphasized and the harmony part should support the melody.
- "Galway" should be pronounced GAHL-weh.
- If the articulation is not as clear as you would like, ask the students to whisper the words in rhythm. Whispering can correct careless articulation.

Evaluation:
(From the student text)
- Circle the other 16th note passages in your music. Are you stressing each 16th note evenly? Listen to the other sections in your choir and evaluate their progress. (*NS* 7A, 7B)
- Listen critically for good, clear diction and clean, crisp articulation. (*NS* 7A, 7B)

Extension:
- As there are no dynamics indicated in the music, lead the class in a discussion of dynamics and decide which phrases should be contrasting.

Piping Tim Of Galway

For TB and Piano

Arranged by
FREDERICK SWANSON

Ev - 'ry per - son in the na - tion,__
When he walks the high-way peal - ing,__

or of great or hum - ble sta - tion,__ Holds in high - est es - ti - ma - tion,
'round his head the birds go wheel - ing.__ Tim has car - ols worth the steal - ing,

Student
Book Page
103

Student
Book Page
105

count - ing_ sleep a thing to scorn._ Old is_ he, but not out-worn,

count - ing_ sleep a thing to scorn. Old is_ he, but not out-worn,

D. S. al ⊕

Pip - ing Tim of Gal - way.

Pip - ing_ Tim of Gal - way.

D. S. al ⊕

⊕ *Coda*

Pip - ing_Tim, Pip - ing_Tim of Gal - way.

Pip - ing_Tim, Pip - ing_Tim of Gal - way.

⊕ *Coda*

Student
Book Page
106

130

ROSALEE

Composer: Dave and Jean Perry
Text: Dave and Jean Perry
Voicing: TTB

Key: G Major
Meter: 6/8
Form: A A B A
Style: Sea Chantey

Accompaniment: Piano
Programming: Concert, festival, or contest

Ranges:

Student
Book Page
107

ROSALEE

Composer: Dave and Jean Perry
Text: Dave and Jean Perry
Voicing: TTB

Cultural Context:
"Rosalee" is a sea *chantey*, a song sung by sailors in rhythm with their work. This chantey speaks of a sailor's wish to return home to his love, Rosalee.

The composers of this original sea chantey are Dave and Jean Perry, a husband and wife song-writing team who live in Arizona. In addition to their writing, they are both choral directors—Jean directs choral groups at the junior high level and Dave is a high school choral director. They have written many choral works for school and church choirs.

Musical Terms:

cresc. (crescendo)	*mf* (mezzo forte)	*f* (forte)
In two ♩ = 100	unison	*no rit.* (no ritardando)

Preparation:
• "Rosalee" is written in 6/8 meter. The stressed syllable is beat 1. Say the following line from "Rosalee," putting the stress on the underlined beats.

• Remember to keep the vowel shapes round and tall. Practice saying the following words using good round vowel sounds.

of = ahv	Rosalee = Roh-sah-lee	the = thah
love = lahv	down = dah(oo)n	

Circle the words printed above in your music to help you remember the vowel shape.

Evaluation:
Chant the last verse of "Rosalee" in rhythm. Do you hear:

• Word stress on beat 1?

• The use of tall vowel sounds?

Objectives:

- The student will develop proper diction through the use of correct vowel shapes. (*National Standard* 1A)
- The student will learn to sing with correct syllabic stress. (*NS* 1E)

Historical/Stylistic Guidelines:

"Rosalee" is a sea chantey. A chantey is a song sung by sailors in rhythm with their work. As Richard Henry Dana wrote in *Two Years Before the Mast*: "A song is as necessary to sailors as the fife and drum to soldiers." These men sang constantly at work, and the rhythmic movement provided by these songs helped the sailors achieve the teamwork necessary for heaving and pulling. A chantey's accents, strength of beat, and rhythmic drive reflected the type of work that was being done.

After the Revolutionary War, the United States began building ships that rivaled any ships built in Europe. New American technology created the clipper which was the unrivaled queen of the seas until it was replaced by the steamboat around 1850.

Vocal Technique/Warm-Ups/Exercises:

"Rosalee" is an excellent piece for the developing boys choir. Each verse begins in unison and moves to a simple three-part chordal structure. Practice the following excerpt from Rosalee the following ways:

- as a sightreading exercise
- on "too"
- on the words

*Isolate this note and practice it with the "yawn sigh" found in *Essential Musicianship* Book I, p.1.

Rehearsal Guidelines and Notes
Suggested Sequence:

1. Familiarize students with the musical terms found in this piece as listed in the student text. (*NS* 5C)
2. Review the material found in the Preparation section of the student page.
3. Chant the words in rhythm to the first two verses (mm. 5-39) and add the pitches as a sight-reading drill. Remind the students to use proper word stress.
4. Introduce the chorus (mm. 39-55) and remind the singers to hold out the sustained notes for the full value.
5. Teach the last verse (mm. 59-75). The bass part has the melody at first, then the melody shifts to the first tenor. Ask the students to find the similarities and differences in their part between this verse and the other two verses.
6. Introduce the final chorus (mm. 75-87) which is a repeat of the first chorus.
7. Teach the last line (mm. 88-91) as a separate unit because the melodic pattern changes.
8. Remind the students to make the most of the dynamic changes and phrase markings indicated in the score.

Performance Tips:

- The key to success with "Rosalee" is an energetic sound with a great deal of intensity in the tone.
- In the "oo" sections in the last verse, remind the singers to keep the vowel very tall. Begin with an "ah" vowel and round the lips to form an "oo." (The back of the mouth should still be an "ah" position.)
- Note that there is no ritard at the end of the piece.
- Remind the singers to keep the stress on beat one. If they are having trouble with this concept, ask them to sway back and forth gently in rhythm until they can feel beat one in every measure.
- When pronouncing "Rosalee," ask the singers to sing "Ro-sah-lee." Be aware that some singers may want to spread the "e" vowel at the end of the word. They can correct this problem by bringing in the corners of the mouth instead of spreading them out. (Some call this the "fish mouth" exercise.)

Evaluation:

- Perform the evaluation as it is found on the student page.
- Chant the last verse of "Rosalee" in rhythm. Do you hear: (*NS 7A, 7B*)

    - Word stress on beat 1?
    - The use of tall vowel sounds?

Extension:

What other sea chanteys can you name? ("Boatmen Stomp," "Blow Ye Winds," and "The Drunken Sailor")

Rosalee

For TTB and Piano

Words and Music by
DAVE and JEAN PERRY

Student
Book Page
108

though I love the sail - ing life, the free - dom of the sea; —— I

though I love the sail - ing life, the free - dom of the sea; —— I

though I love the sail - ing life, the free - dom of the sea; —— I

cresc

love it most when we set sail for home and Ros - a - lee.

cresc

love it most when we set sail for home and Ros - a - lee.

cresc

love it most when we set sail for home and Ros - a - lee.

f

mf

Student
Book Page
109

135

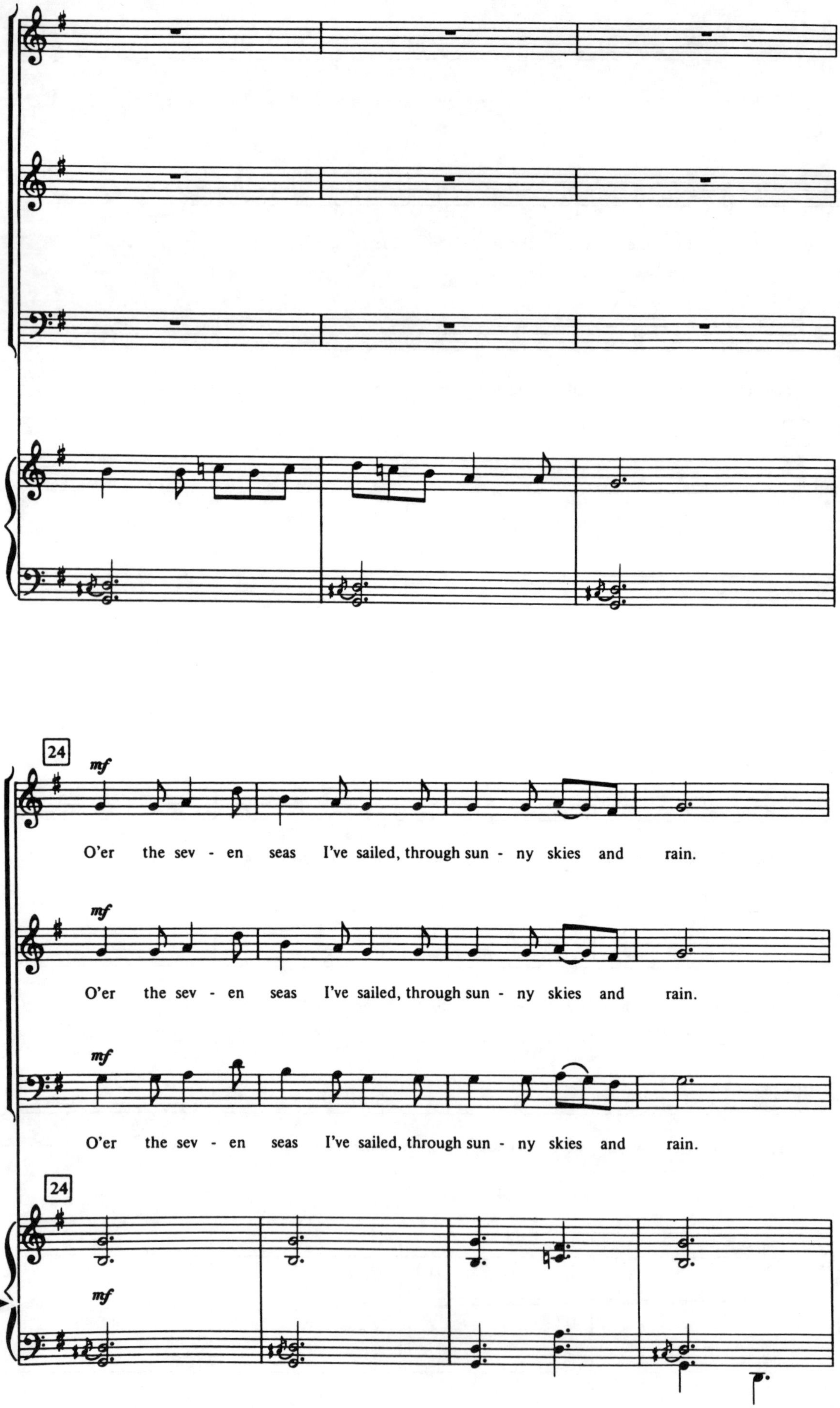

O'er the sev - en seas I've sailed, through sun - ny skies and rain.

O'er the sev - en seas I've sailed, through sun - ny skies and rain.

O'er the sev - en seas I've sailed, through sun - ny skies and rain.

Student Book Page 110

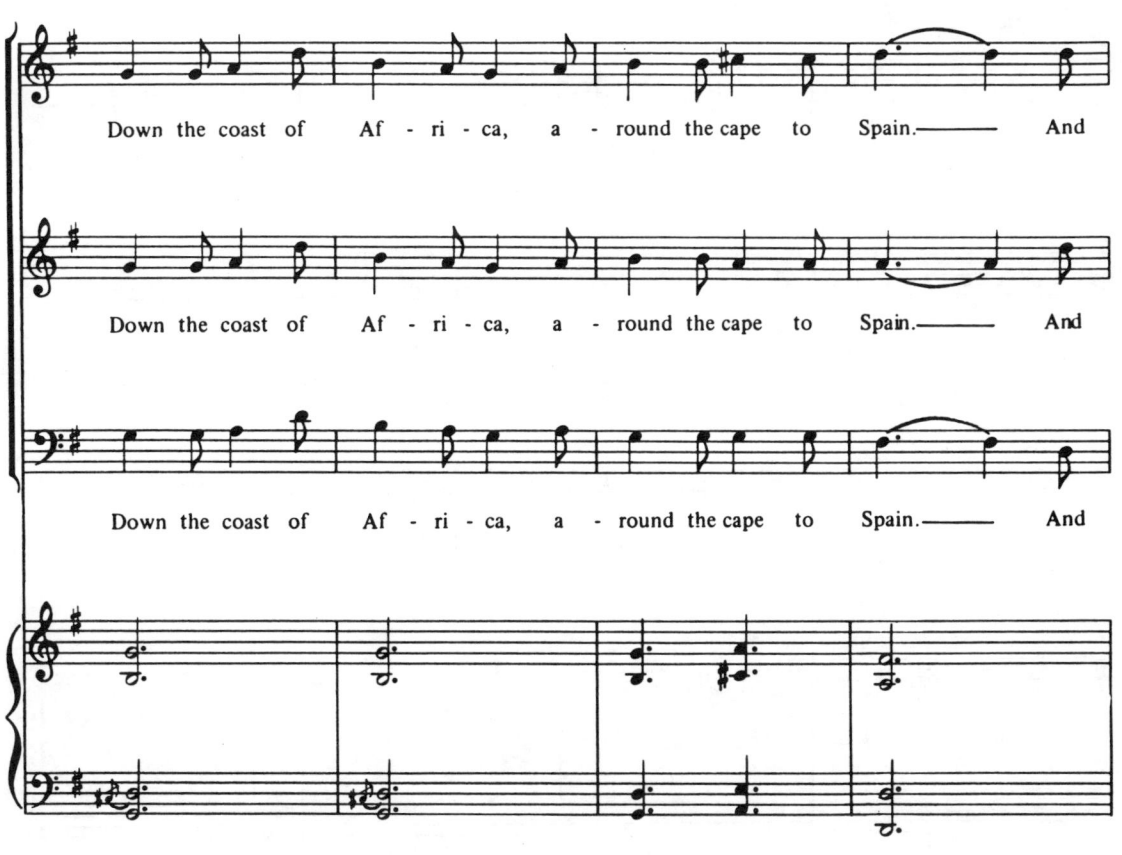

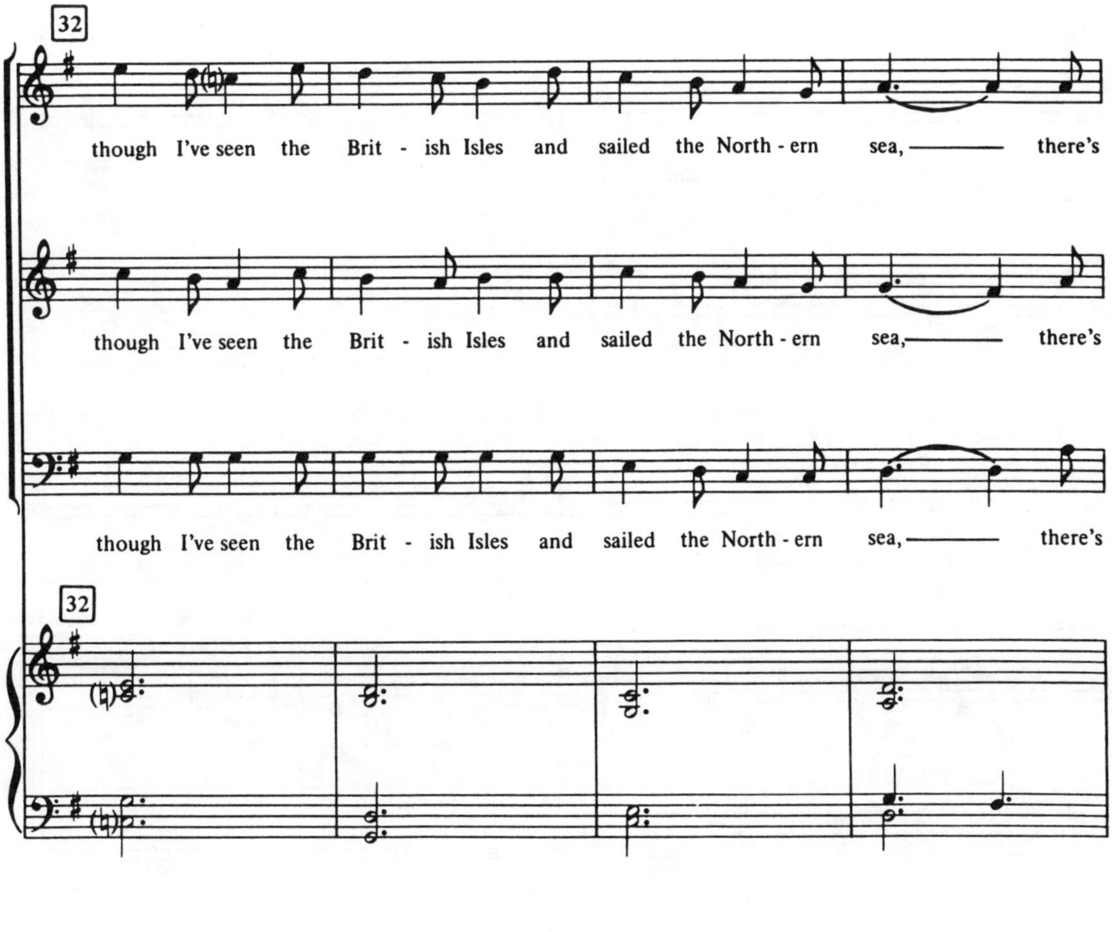

Down the coast of Af - ri - ca, a - round the cape to Spain.———— And

Down the coast of Af - ri - ca, a - round the cape to Spain.———— And

Down the coast of Af - ri - ca, a - round the cape to Spain.———— And

though I've seen the Brit - ish Isles and sailed the North - ern sea,———— there's

though I've seen the Brit - ish Isles and sailed the North - ern sea,———— there's

though I've seen the Brit - ish Isles and sailed the North - ern sea,———— there's

Student Book Page 111

not a place I'd rath-er be than home with Ros - a - lee. Ros - a -

not a place I'd rath-er be than home with Ros - a - lee.

not a place I'd rath-er be than home with Ros - a - lee.

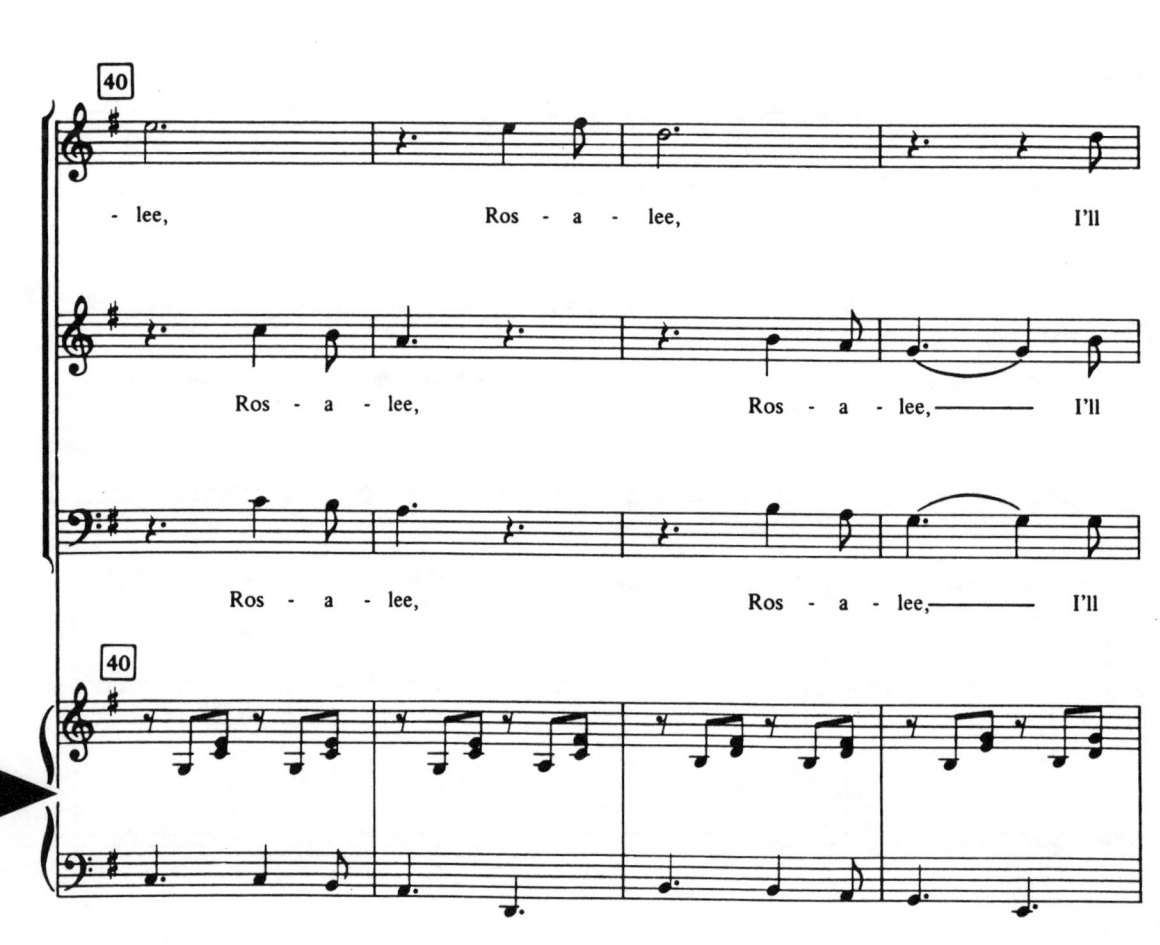

- lee, Ros - a - lee, I'll

Ros - a - lee, Ros - a - lee,————— I'll

Ros - a - lee, Ros - a - lee,————— I'll

soon be sail-in' home a-cross the storm — y sea. Ros-a-

soon be sail-in' home a-cross the storm — y sea.

soon be sail-in' home a-cross the storm — y sea.

-lee, Ros - a, -Ros - a - lee,——— I'm

Ros - a - lee, Ros - a - lee,——— I'm

Ros - a - lee, Ros - a - lee,——— I'm

Student Book Page 113

com - in' back to see my Ros - a - lee.

com - in' back to see my Ros - a - lee.

com - in' back to see my Ros - a - lee.

mf

The

mf

A

A

clip - per ship I'm sail - in' is the fin - est of her kind.———

brav - er crew and cap - tain you'll like - ly nev - er find.——— Her

brav - er crew and cap - tain you'll like - ly nev - er find.———

oo ——— oo ——— You'll like - ly nev - er find.———

Student
Book Page
115

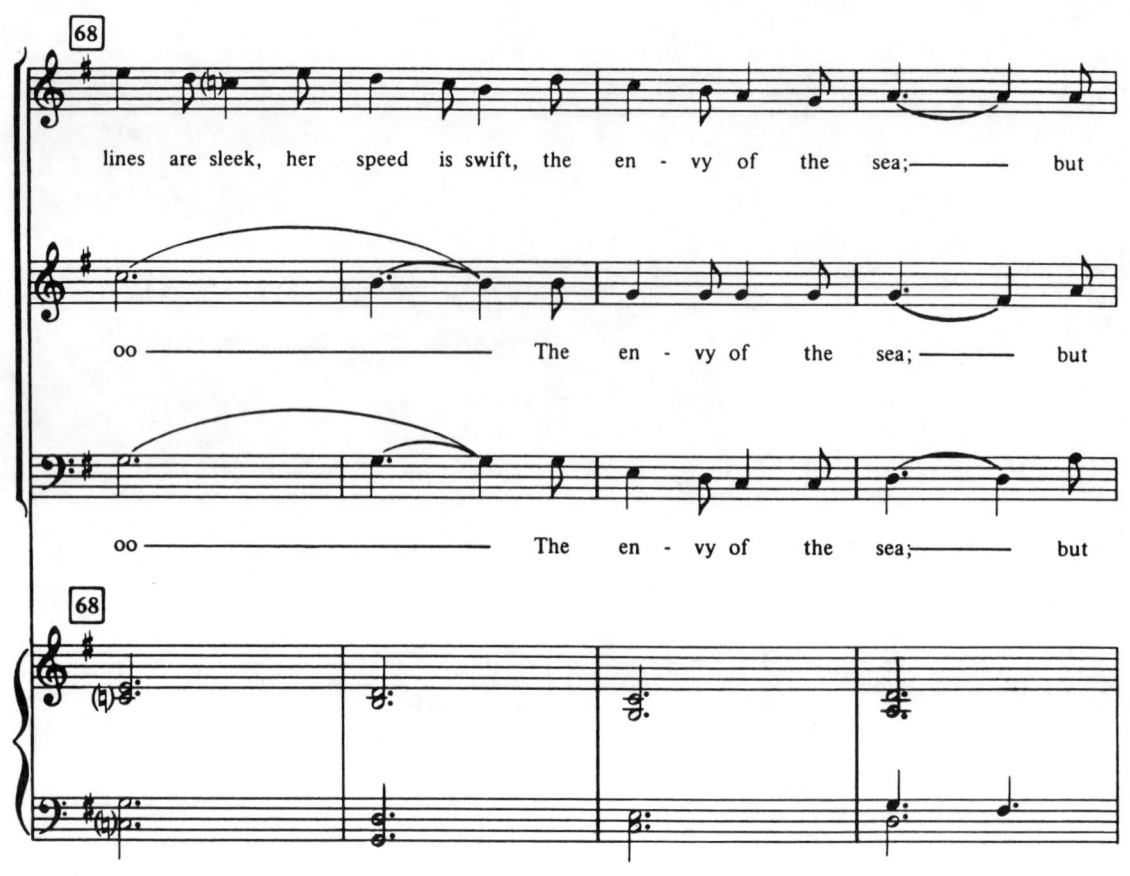

lines are sleek, her speed is swift, the en - vy of the sea;——— but

oo ——————————— The en - vy of the sea;——— but

oo ——————————— The en - vy of the sea;——— but

though she's fine she can't com-pare to home and Ros - a - lee. Ros - a -

though she's fine she can't com-pare to home and Ros - a - lee.

though she's fine she can't com-pare to home and Ros - a - lee.

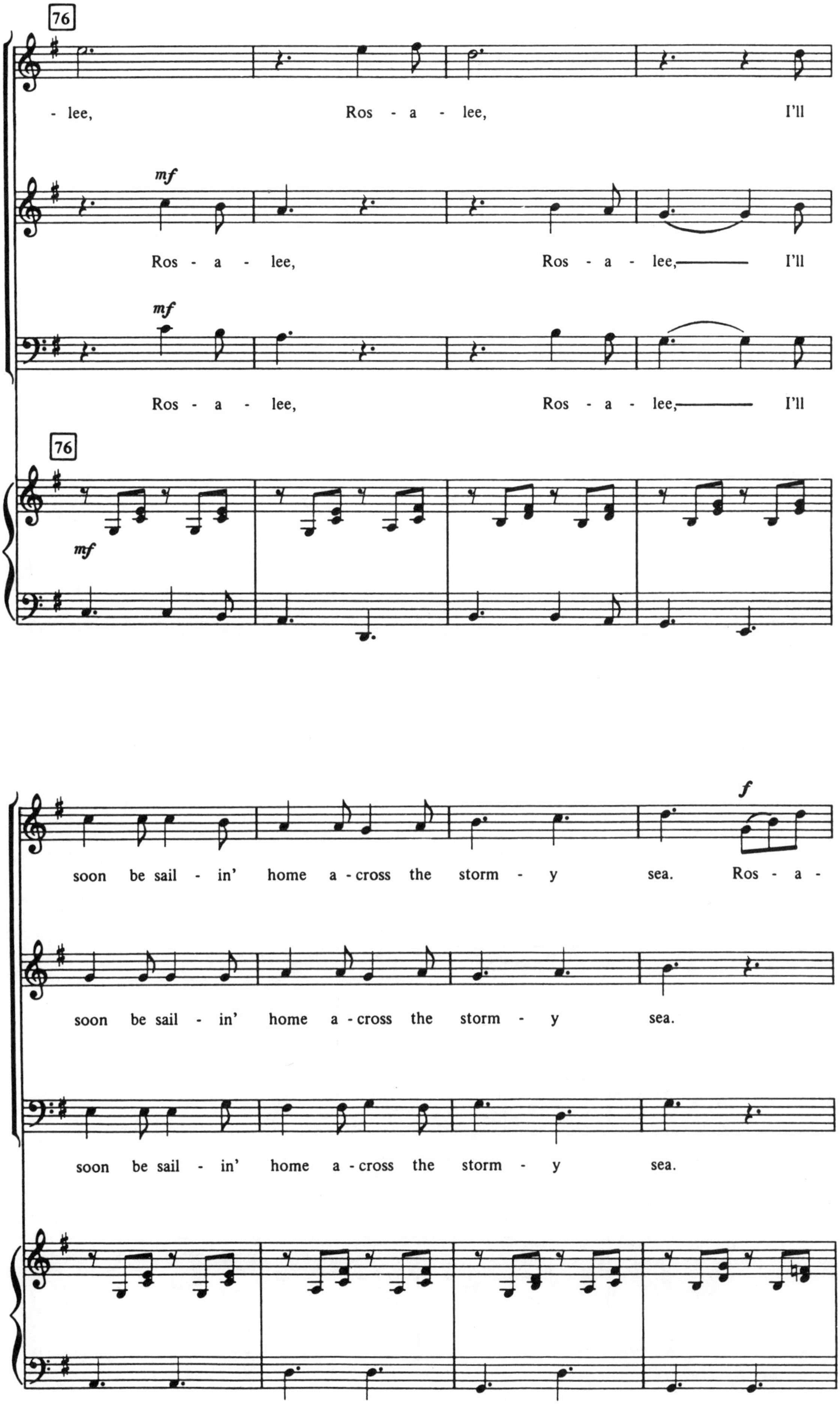

76 - lee, Ros - a - lee, I'll

Ros - a - lee, Ros - a - lee,——— I'll

Ros - a - lee, Ros - a - lee,——— I'll

soon be sail - in' home a - cross the storm - y sea. Ros - a -

soon be sail - in' home a - cross the storm - y sea.

soon be sail - in' home a - cross the storm - y sea.

Student
Book Page
117

Student Book Page 118

SANSA KROMA

Composer: African Game Song, arranged by Emily Crocker

Text: Traditional

Voicing: TBB(B) a cappella

Key: F Major

Meter: ¢

Form: A A B A coda

Style: African Game Song

Accompaniment: a cappella voices with percussion instruments: high/low drums, claves

Programming: Multicultural program or festival, concert

Ranges:

Student Book Page 119

SANSA KROMA

Composer: African Game Song, arranged by Emily Crocker

Text: Traditional

Voicing: TTB (opt. TTBB) a cappella

Cultural Context:

This African game song may be performed with a variety of percussion instruments. Experiment with different sounds and rhythm patterns to create an interesting accompaniment. Add hand claps and step the beat to involve the entire body in creating the music. The words mean "Sansa, the hawk. You are an orphan so you kidnap the little chicks."

Musical Terms:

($\downarrow$ = ca. 84)

div. (divisi)

dim. (diminuendo)

f (forte)

‖: :‖ (repeat signs)

poco a poco

unis. (unison)

> (accent)

p (piano)

Preparation:

Practice these rhythm patterns by snapping, clapping, or tapping. Try each one separately, then all together.

Evaluation:

After you have learned the notes, rhythm, and words to this song, add percussion instruments (if available). Decide which actions (hand claps, step touches, snaps) you will add. Video tape the choir performing this song with the instruments and actions. Was the beat steady and the rhythms correct?

145

Objectives:

- The student will perform literature and discuss characteristics of African folk music. (*National Standard* 1E)
- The student will develop rhythmic accuracy and expand rhythmic reading skills. (*NS* 1E)

Historical/Stylistic Guidelines:

"Sansa Kroma" is an African folk song (playground game) sung by village children in the region of Ghana. It tells a reassuring story of how young animals in the wild are often orphaned and must survive on their own, but that children need not worry for if orphaned they will be taken in and cared for by relatives and friends.

Word pronunciation is as follows:

Sansa kroma ne neh woo awcheche kokoma.

Sahn-zah kroh-mah nee neh woo aw-chee-chee koh-koh-mah

Vocal Technique/Warm-Ups/Exercises:

- For vocal warm-up and chord tuning practice, rehearse the following exercise each day before singing "Sanza Kroma." These chords are found in the B section of the song (m. 29).

- Review and practice the rhythm patterns found in the Preparation section on the student page. Check that the two dotted quarter notes are accurately performed.

Rehearsal Guidelines and Notes
Suggested Sequence:

1. Familiarize students with the musical terms found in this piece as listed in the student text. (*NS* 5C)

2. Present and discuss the cultural/historical background of this song. Prepare an overhead transparency or handout of the rhythm exercises, the chord progressions, and the word pronunciation guide. Practice these before starting the music.

3. Teach by sections, set apart by the repeat signs, in this sequence:

   - Chant the words in rhythm.
   - Sing the pitches for each part separately, then combine.

4. Perform the song utilizing all dynamic markings indicated in the score. Add percussion as you wish.

Performance Tips:

- This song must be performed with hard, crisp consonants to accentuate the rhythmic drive and to give it energy.
- If the low F's are out of range (too low) for the First Tenors, ask them to merely mouth the words rather than force the sound or sing out of tune.
- Allow extra time to work on the tuning of the chords in the B section (m.28-44). They are vital to the success of this piece.
- Exaggerate the *dim. poco a poco* at the end. Create a gradual fade-out by singing each "Sansa . ." a little softer then *forte* on the last two measures. Careful that the singers do not yell or oversing the ending.
- Add a simple step-touch dance step or other rhythmic motions to the performance.

Evaluation:

Evaluate the student's progress by making a video tape of the class performing this song. Watch the tape with the class. Have every singer complete this checklist:

- Were the rhythms performed correctly?

  ___ always ___ mostly ___ not at all

- Were the consonants hard and crisp?

  ___ always ___ mostly ___ not at all

- Did the performance express rhythmic drive and energy?

  ___ always ___ mostly ___ not at all

- Were the chords sung in tune in the B section?

  ___ always ___ mostly ___ not at all

- Was the dynamic contrast obvious in the last 8 measures?

  ___ always ___ mostly ___ not at all

Extension:

- Ask students to bring recordings or tapes of other African folk music from their homes, the local library, or area cultural center.
- Compose a rhythm ensemble using classroom instruments with the Preparation exercises as a model. (*NS 1A*)

Sansa Kroma

For TTB(B) and Percussion

This African game song may be performed with a variety of percussion instruments. Experiment with different sounds and rhythm patterns to create an interesting accompaniment. Add hand claps and step the beat to involve the entire body in creating the music. The words mean: "Sansa, the hawk. You are an orphan so you kidnap the little chicks."

African Game Song
Arranged by EMILY CROCKER

Student Book Page 120

Student
Book Page
121

149

Lower notes are optional through meas. 44.

San - sa, __ san - sa, __

san - sa, __ san - sa. __

Solo or group

San - sa kro - ma ne neh woo aw - che - che ko - ko - ma,

San - sa, __ san - sa, __

san - sa kro - ma ne neh woo aw-che-che ko-ko - ma.

san - sa, ___ san - sa. ___

dim.

49 Unis.

mf

San - sa kro - ma ne neh woo aw-che-che ko-ko - ma,

mf

mf

Student Book Page 123

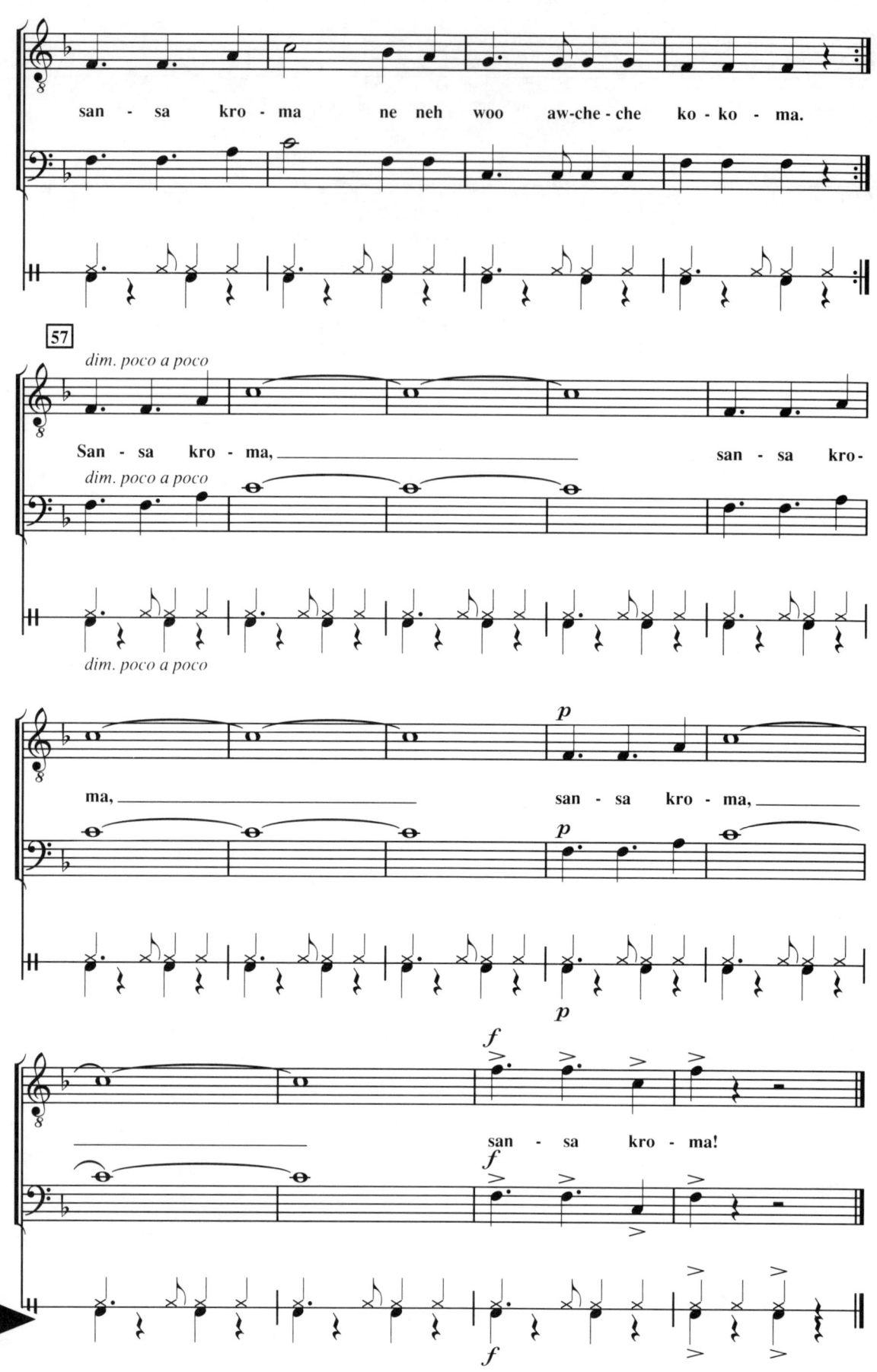

san - sa kro - ma   ne neh woo   aw-che - che   ko - ko - ma.

57

dim. poco a poco

San - sa   kro - ma, _____   san - sa   kro -

dim. poco a poco

dim. poco a poco

ma, _____   *p*   san - sa   kro - ma, _____

p

p

f   san - sa   kro - ma!

f

f

CHORALE FROM *SLEEPERS AWAKE* (Cantata No. 140, *Wachet Auf*)

Composer: Johann Sebastian Bach (1685-1750), arranged by Emily Crocker

Text: Based on Biblical New Testament texts

Voicing: TB

Ranges:

Key: E♭ Major
Meter: 4/4
Form: Binary
Style: Baroque contrapuntal style
Accompaniment: Piano

Programming: Contest or festival, concert; good piece for teaching Baroque style.

Student Book Page 125

CHORALE FROM *SLEEPERS AWAKE* (Cantata No. 140, *Wachet Auf*)

Composer: Johann Sebastian Bach (1685-1750), arranged by Emily Crocker
Text: Based on Biblical New Testament texts
Voicing: TB

Cultural Context:
"Sleepers Awake" is the chorale from a cantata of the same title. A cantata is a composition for choir, soloists, organ, and sometimes orchestra that is written as part of a church service. Bach wrote at least 295 cantatas at the amazing rate of one cantata per week! Unfortunately, many of these are now lost. *Sleepers Awake* survives today and is among the most well-known of Bach's cantatas.

Musical Terms:
(♩ = ca. 72) *mf* (mezzo forte) (decrescendo)

(crescendo) *mp* (mezzo piano) *f* (forte)

tr (trill) suspension resolution

Preparation:
One of the challenges of this piece is learning to sing *suspensions*. A suspension occurs when two voices move to a whole or half step apart. As one voice stays the same, the other *resolves* (moves up or down). Practice suspensions and resolutions with this exercise.

Suspension Practice:

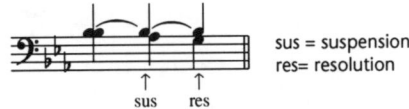

sus = suspension
res = resolution

sus res

More Complicated Suspension Practice:

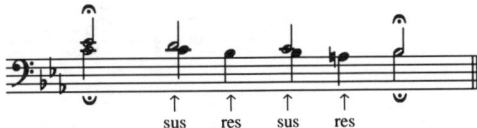

sus res sus res

Now you are ready for the suspensions in "Sleepers Awake." Can you find where they occur?

Evaluation:
After you have learned "Sleepers Awake," tape record your choir slowly singing measures. 14-20 a cappella. Now listen to your tape and choose the statement below that best describes what you heard in the spots with suspensions.

• Pitches were exactly correct. Each part held their own pitch.

• One part tended to pull the other part to that pitch.

• Both parts got mixed-up on pitches.

(Answers to student page questions)
Suspensions occur in mm. 18, 21, 39, 42, and 69.

Objectives:

- The student will increase ability to sing in tune while singing suspensions. (*National Standard* 1E)
- The student will develop proper German diction through the correct use of vowel shapes and syllabic stress. (*NS* 1A)
- The student will perform choral literature of the Baroque era. (*NS* 6B, 9A)

Historical/Stylistic Guidelines:

Review the Cultural Context information in the student page.

Cantatas, especially those of Johann Sebastian Bach, are considered of enormous musical worth. Donald Grout, in *A History of Western Music* (p. 395) notes that "no generalized description can possibly suggest the infinite variety, the inconceivable wealth of musical invention, technical mastery, and religious devotion in Bach's cantatas."

The cantata is written as functional music for weekly church services with texts based on the scripture lesson of the day. There is no story line, but each cantata has a unifying thought or theme. Bach's cantatas ranged in length from 12 to 40 minutes, usually opening and ending with a chorus, interspersed with recitatives, arias, duets, trios, instrumental interludes, etc.

Wachet Auf was written in 1731 for the 27th Sunday after Trinity. The text is based on the New Testament parable (Matthew 25:1-13 and Mark 13:34) of the wise and foolish maidens and the arrival of the bridegroom for whom they are preparing the lamps. The melody is based on a familiar hymn-tune with music and words written by the mystic poet-composer Philipp Nicolai (1556-1608) in 1599. The three verses of the hymn-tune occur at the beginning, middle, and end of the cantata. Between each presentation of the chorale appear a duet and a recitative. (1. Chorus, 2. Tenor recitative, 3. Duet for soprano and baritone, 4. Tenor section of Chorus, 5. Baritone recitative, 6. Duet for soprano and baritone, and 7. Chorale).

The famous 4th section, upon which this arrangement is based, was originally written to be sung by unison tenors, and as such is essentially a trio for tenor voices, strings, and basso continuo. Ms. Crocker's arrangement remains very true to the original, with the addition of an optional baritone part.

Vocal Technique/Warm-Ups/Exercises:

- Perform the Preparation exercise on the student page as a warm-up and tuning exercise for the suspensions in "Sleepers Awake."
- Practice phrasing using the following exercise based on the opening phrase of the piece.

    - Sing on a neutral syllable; move the exercise up and/or down by half steps as a warm-up.

    - Remind the students not to change pitch as they crescendo.

    - Sing the words in the score using the same technique.

Rehearsal Guidelines and Notes
Suggested Sequence:

1. Familiarize students with the musical terms found in this piece as listed in the student text. (*NS* 5C)
2. Chant the rhythm of mm. 13-22. Pay special attention to mm. 18 and 21, chanting each voice part separately.
3. Sightread the pitches of mm. 13-22, then note that identical pitches appear in mm. 34-43.
4. Learn the last two sections (mm. 50-57 and m. 70) following the same procedures.

5. When students can sing the entire song accurately using neutral syllables, add the accompaniment. It may be effective if singers listen to the accompaniment first, before adding their parts, or listen to a professional recording to note the relationship between singers and accompaniment.

6. Finally, teach the words. German is preferred because of authenticity and word stress.

7. Rehearse the entire work, paying particular attention to tone quality and phrasing.

German: *Zion hört die Wächter singen*
Pronunciation: TSEE-ahn huȓt dee VECH-tehȓ ZING-ehn

        das Herz tut ihr von Freude springen,
        dahs hehȓts toot eeȓ fawn FR̃OH(ee)-deh SHPRING-ehn

        sie wachet und steht eilend auf.
        zee VAH-cheht oont SHTEH(ee)t AH(ee)-lehnt AH(oo)f

        Ihr Freund kommt von Himmel prächtig von Gnaden stark,
        eeȓ FR̃OH(ee)nd kohmt fawn HIHM-mehl PR̃EHCH-teeg fawn G'NAH-dehn shtahȓk

        von Wahrheit mächtig, ihr Licht wird hell, ihr Stern geht auf.
        fawn VAHR̃-hah(ee)t MECH-teeg eeȓ leecht* veeȓt hehl eeȓ shtehȓn GEH(ee)t AH(oo)f

        Nun komm, du werte Kron, Herr Jesu Gottes Sohn. Hosianna!
        noon kohm doo VEHR̃-teh Kȓohn hehȓ YEH-zoo GAW-tehs zohn hoh-zee-AH-nah

        Wir folgen All zum Freuden Saal
        veeȓ FOHL-gehn Ahl tsoom FR̃OH(ee)-dehn zahl

        und halten mit das Abendmahl.
        oont HAHL-tehn miht dahs AH-behnt-mahl

                                     *ȓ = rolled or flipped r
ch = same sound as when saying "Bach"
consult a German expert for correct pronunciation

Performance Tips:

- Try using harpsichord accompaniment if available; it is authentic to this time period and blends well with boys' voices.
- Modify the tenor part as needed to accommodate those who cannot sing the low E-flats (m. 13 and elsewhere). In most cases, tenors can mouth the words and the part can be carried by the basses for one or two notes. Refer to the cued notes in the tenor line (m. 13 for example).
- Emphasize legato line, blended tone, and intensity throughout a phrase in this piece.
- Note that the editor has included helpful crescendo and decrescendo markings. These should imply an increasing phrase intensity appropriate for Baroque pieces, rather than large changes in loudness which might be more appropriate for another style.

Evaluation:

- Complete the Evaluation as specified on the student page. (*NS 7A, 7B*)
- Assess the singers' ability to increase intensity across a phrase without changing the pitch by using the warm-up exercise in the Vocal Technique section of the teacher's edition as an evaluation tool. Record the choir singing the exercise by section. The director or remaining section can then evaluate. Reverse tasks. (*NS 7A, 7B*)

Extension:

- Listen to a recording of *Wachet Auf*, paying particular attention to the 4th section.
- Suggest that singers report on one of the following:

    J.S. Bach
    Cantata
    Wachet Auf
    Harpsichord
    Famous children of J.S. Bach
    Chorale
    Life during the Baroque time period (1600-1750)

Chorale from

Sleepers Awake

For TB and Piano

This famous movement from Bach's cantata was originally for tenor solo. While the original key has been retained in this arrangement, the baritone part has been added and is optional.

By JOHANN SEBASTIAN BACH
Arranged by EMILY CROCKER

Student Book Page 126

Student
Book Page
127

und steht __ ei - lend __ auf.
ru - sa - lem, __ a - rise!

und steht ei - lend __ auf.
ru - sa - lem, __ a - rise!

mf

p

159

hell, ihr ___ Stern _ geht auf.
come, his ___ star _ now shines.

hell, ihr Stern _ geht _ auf.
come, his star _ now _ shines.

Nun
Now

Nun
Now

Student Book Page 130

komm, du wer - te Kron,
come O bless - ed one,
Herr Je - su
the Fath - er's

komm, du wer - te Kron,
come O bless - ed one,
Herr Je - su
the Fath - er's

Got - tes Sohn.
on - ly son.
Ho - si - an -
Ho - san -

Got - tes Sohn.
on - ly son.
Ho - si - an -
Ho - san -

na!
na!

na!
na!

Student
Book Page
131

162

163

THIS TRAIN

Composer: Traditional Spiritual, arranged by Roger Emerson
Text: Traditional
Voicing: TTB

Key: F minor
Meter: $\frac{4}{4}$
Form: Strophic with added interlude and coda
Style: Traditional spiritual arranged in pop style

Accompaniment: Piano with optional rhythm section
Programming: Concert opener or closer; audience favorite

Ranges:

Student Book Page 134

THIS TRAIN

Composer: Traditional Spiritual, arranged by Roger Emerson
Text: Traditional
Voicing: TTB

Cultural Context:
"This Train," like several other familiar spirituals, may have had two meanings. In one meaning, the train is on its way to heaven ("This train is bound for glory."). In a second, the words to "This Train" may have had hidden meaning for slaves longing for freedom and safety. Perhaps the "train" is the Underground Railroad.

The arranger of this piece, Roger Emerson, is well-known for his contemporary settings of traditional spirituals. Notice the interesting harmonies in the piano underneath the solid vocal lines.

Musical Terms:

($\downarrow$ = 144)   *mf* (mezzo forte)   *p* (piano)

⟨ (crescendo)   ⟩ (decrescendo)   *mp* (mezzo piano)

N.B. (no breath)   (accent)

Preparation:
The challenge of this song is to sing with crisp diction. Practice this skill with this exercise:

This train don't carry no gamblers,
This train is bound for glory,
Don't carry no-one but the righteous and the holy.

1. Speak it slowly and clearly together as a group. Pay special attention to ending consonants.

2. Speak it faster and clearly together as a group.

3. Speak the words precisely, but do not get louder. Just emphasize the consonants more strongly.

Evaluation:
After you have learned the pitches and rhythms of "This Train," listen to your choir sing this song a cappella (either on tape or live). As you listen, underline each consonant in your part that cannot be obviously heard. Your music might look like this:

Don'<u>t</u> carry no-o<u>n</u>e bu<u>t</u> the righteous and the holy.

These underlines should be reminders to pay special attention to diction in these spots. You may want to do this at various times as you learn this piece and your diction gets better and better.

Objectives:

- The student will develop clear diction to convey the meaning of the text. (*National Standard* 1A)
- The student will demonstrate the ability to blend with other ensemble voices utilizing appropriate tone quality, diction, and intonation. (*NS* 5C)
- The student will perform contemporary choral literature. (*NS* 1E)

Historical/Stylistic Guidelines:

Traditional spirituals, such as this one, are now well known to Americans of all ages. As David Ewen observed in *All the Years of American Popular Music* (p. 35), "It is impossible to exaggerate the influence of the Negro song on American popular music."

Spirituals were not always an accepted part of American culture, however. Not until 1871 did the spiritual first come into general popularity due to the efforts of "The Jubilee Singers," a group from Fisk University in Nashville. The Jubilee Singers, under the direction of George L. White, began touring the country in an effort to raise money for the struggling Fisk University. They gave concerts devoted exclusively to what would later be called spirituals. White was given permission to tour, but only on the condition that he himself would defray all expenses. Nine young singers began that tour in 1871, "fighting cold and starvation, shut out of hotels, and scornfully sneered at, ever northward; and ever the magic of their song kept thrilling hearts, until a burst of applause at the Congregational Council at Oberlin revealed them to the world. They came to New York and Henry Ward Beecher (abolitionist preacher and brother of Harriet Beecher Stowe, author of *Uncle Tom's Cabin*) dared to welcome them, even though the metropolitan dailies sneered" using words that we now call obscene. By the time they returned home in 1878 with the vast sum of $15,000.00, "the spiritual had captured the heart of the world."

Vocal Technique/Warm-Ups/Exercises:

- Emphasize beginning and ending consonants using the exercise on the student page as a warm-up.
- An additional warm-up useful for emphasizing diction follows:

ARTICULATE AGILITY'S A MARVELOUS ABILITY!

- Speak syllables very slowly; gradually increasing speed.
- Encourage singers to exaggerate the movement of their lip muscles.
- Vary the dynamics as well as the tempo. Remind students that *piano* articulation takes more energy than *forte* articulation. Do not always pair *forte* with fast, or singers will always tend to sing fast passages loudly.
- Review the articulation section of *Essential Musicianship, Book I*, p. 52.

Rehearsal Guidelines and Notes
Suggested Sequence:

1. Familiarize students with the musical terms found in this piece as listed in the student text. (*NS* 5C)
2. Teach the rhythm of the first verse (mm. 5-19), then teach the pitches.
3. Remind the singers that verses one, two (mm. 21-35) and three (mm. 53-67) are virtually identical except for rhythmic differences created by the text. Teach these verses first.
4. Finally work on the interlude (mm. 37-52) and the coda (mm. 69-end) which are somewhat similar. The most difficult three-part singing occurs in these sections.
5. When all pitches are secure, add accompaniment. Let students listen to the accompaniment alone before attempting to add it to their harmonies.
6. Remind the chorus to pay particular attention to the dynamics and tempo markings indicated in the score.

Performance Tips:

- Add accompaniment only after parts are learned.
- Hold all notes full value and increase in intensity across held notes.
- Dynamic contrasts cannot be over-emphasized, but remind students to avoid oversinging. Instead, ask them to increase the contrast by performing the *piano* parts softer rather than singing the *forte* sections louder to avoid a "shouting" sound.
- Pay special attention to the "No Breath" markings (as in m. 38 and elsewhere).
- On the phrase "This train is bound for glory, this train" increase the intensity on the "ry" of "glory" to eliminate the feeling of pause or breath in the middle of that phrase.
- This piece is very accessible because of the limited ranges and frequent repetition.
- Take extra care on the last 3 measures so that the ending divisi is effective.
- Dynamic contrasts will contribute greatly to a successful performance of this piece.

Evaluation:

- Check diction of consonants by completing the Evaluation section on the student page. (*NS* 7A, 7B)
- Perform the last page a cappella, and check pitches at the end to see if the singers are maintaining intonation while making dynamic changes. Check periodically for progress as you are learning this piece. (*NS* 7A, 7B)

Extension:

Invite chorus members, singers from the area high schools, or members of the community to sing solo arrangements of spirituals such as those by Henry T. Burleigh. Discuss the freedom of interpretation available to a soloist versus a chorus member. (*NS* 6B)

This Train

For TTB and Piano with Optional Rhythm Section

Traditional Spiritual
Arranged by ROGER EMERSON

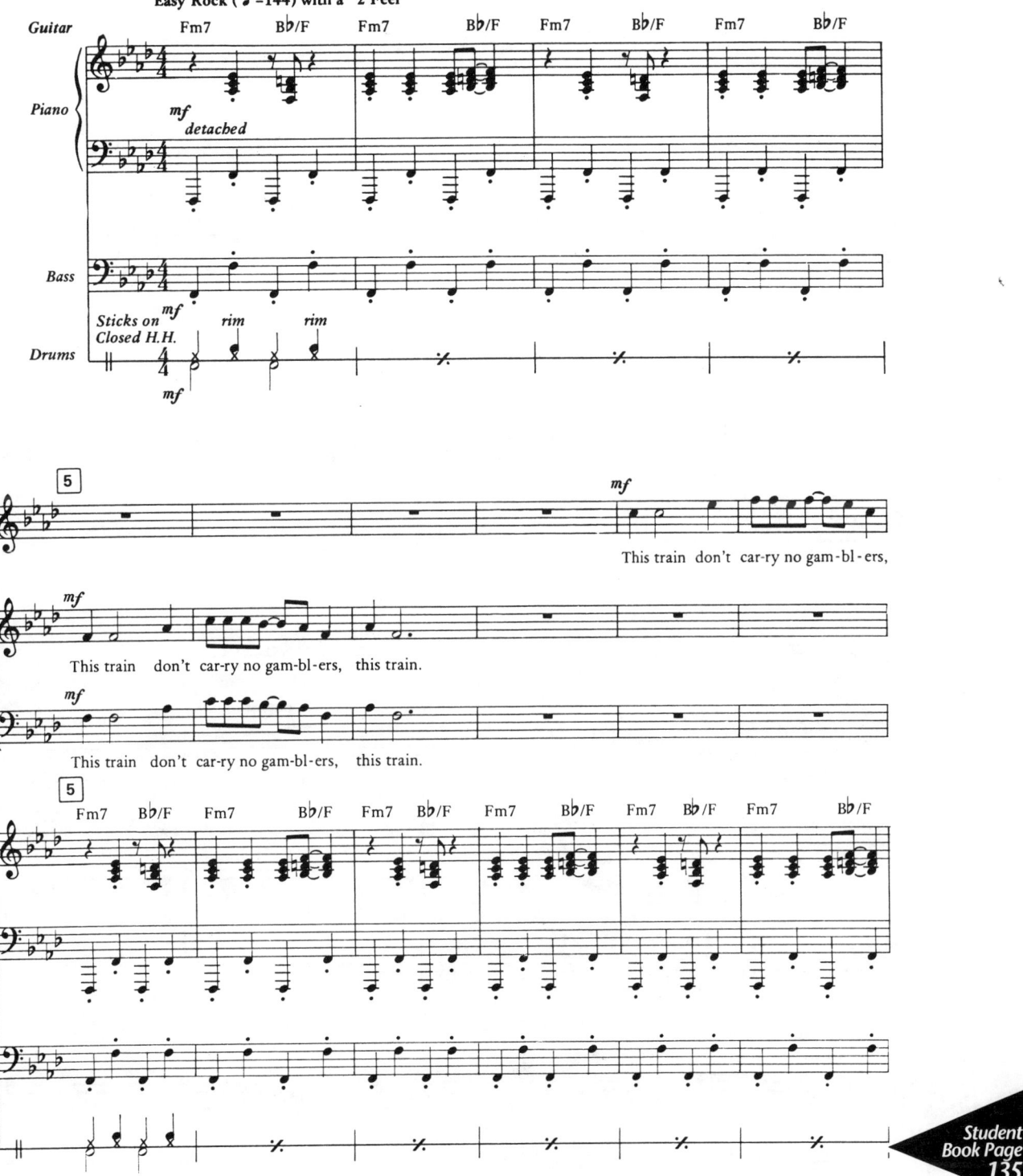

*All boys whose ranges allow sing here.

168

*All boys whose ranges allow sing here.

*All boys whose ranges allow sing here.

Student
Book Page
139

173

VIVA TUTTI

Composer: Traditional Glee, edited by Emily Crocker

Text: Traditional Italian, English lyrics by Emily Crocker

Voicing: TTB

Key: A♭ Major

Meter: 2/4

Form: Sectional

Style: Secular, polyphonic glee

Accompaniment: a cappella

Programming: Contest or festival, concert

Ranges:

Student Book Page 142

VIVA TUTTI (HERE'S TO BEAUTY)

Composer: Traditional Glee, edited by Emily Crocker
Text: Traditional Italian, English lyrics by Emily Crocker
Voicing: TTB a cappella

Cultural Context:
Originally a "glee" was an a cappella partsong sung by men. Large college organizations developed "Glee Clubs" in which men met and sang songs like "Viva Tutti." Probably the most famous Glee Club was the Harvard Glee Club, at Harvard University in Cambridge, Massachusetts. Glee Club songs were usually not serious and were meant to be enjoyed by those singing them. Because they were sung by college men, they were often in a foreign language (often in Latin, but in this case, Italian). When you prepare to sing this song, you are joining a long line of men who have rehearsed, sung, and enjoyed "Viva Tutti."

Musical Terms:

non legato	(♩ = ca. 100)	*mf* (mezzo forte)
‾♪ (tenuto)	‾>♪ (accent)	*mp* (mezzo piano
cresc. (crescendo)	*f* (forte)	_____ (decrescendo)
_____ (crescendo)	♪• (staccato)	*sub.* (subito)
p (piano)	al fine	*no rit.* (no ritardando)

Preparation:
Prepare to learn the Italian in this song by reading the following aloud:

Italian:
Pronunciation:

Viva tutti levezzose,
VEE-vah TOO-tee leh-veh-TZAW-zeh

Donne a'mabiliamo rose,
DAWN-neh ah-mah-BEE-l(ee)ah-maw ŘAW-zeh

Che non anno crudelta,
keh nawn AH-naw křoo-DEHL-tah

Viva sempre, delle donne sol de riva,
VEE-vah SEHM-přeh DEHL-leh DAWN-neh sawl deh ŘEE-vah

Labramata sedelta.
lah-břah-MAH-tah seh-DEHL-tah

*řr = flipped or rolled r.

Evaluation:
Can you speak Italian vowels without "Americanizing" them?

• Slowly speak "Le-vez-zo-se." Did the last "e" sound like " eh" or "ay"? Which should it be?

• Sing the first 8 measures of "Viva Tutti" with your choir. Did each phrase end in "eh" or "ay"?

You are really getting the idea of Italian if you can sing "roseh" and not "rosay." Good luck. This will take some practice and concentration.

(Answers to Evaluation)
Levezzose should end in "eh" not "ay."

174

Objectives:

- The student will develop proper Italian diction through the correct use of vowel shapes and syllabic stress. (*National Standard* 1A)

- The student will demonstrate the ability to blend with other ensemble voices utilizing appropriate tone quality, diction, and intonation. (*NS* 5C)

Historical/Stylistic Guidelines:

To explain the term "glee," read and discuss the Cultural Context section of the student page.

Emily Crocker, a native Texan, was a professional educator for fifteen years. She taught all levels of choral music, specializing in middle school/junior high, where her choirs received numerous superior ratings in concert and sight-reading competitions. In 1989, she joined the music publishing industry and is now Director of Choral Publications for Hal Leonard Corporation, Milwaukee, Wisconsin. She holds degrees from the University of North Texas and Texas Woman's University, and has done additional post-graduate work at the University of North Texas where she was assistant conductor of the A Cappella Choir and taught elementary music education classes.

Ms. Crocker is known nationally as one of the premier choral writers specializing in music for young choirs. She has over 100 works currently in print, and since 1986 has been awarded ASCAP special awards for educational and concert music. Her works can be found on contest lists throughout the United States, and each year she receives invitations to write commissioned works.

Vocal Technique/Warm-Ups/Exercises:

After singers have learned "Viva Tutti," practice word stress differentiation using the following exercise:

- Sing on a neutral syllable (doo or too) at a moderate tempo.

- Each time through, accent a different beat. The first time accent only the first beat of each measure; the second time accent only the second half of the first beat of each measure, etc. This will allow the singers to practice placing different accents on different beats in the measure.

- When singers can perform the exercise successfully, ask them to transfer the same skill to the Italian on mm. 5-8.

- Eventually the director should be able to ask singers to accent any syllable and they will have the control to successfully complete the task.

Rehearsal Guidelines and Notes
Suggested Sequence:

1. Familiarize students with the musical terms found in this piece as listed in the student text. (*NS* 5C)

2. Chant the rhythms for each voice part. Once mm. 1-32 are mastered, the remainder of the song is a direct repetition.

3. Teach pitches on neutral or sight-reading syllables. "Viva Tutti" is a good piece to sight-read because of few accidentals and skips.

4. When rhythm and pitch are secure, learn Italian words by rote. See the Preparation section on the student page for an Italian Pronunciation Guide.

5. Remind the students to pay particular attention to the dynamics and phrase markings indicated in the score.

Performance Tips:

- Direct singer's attention to enunciation of Italian words ending in "e." Americans tend to sing them "ay" rather than the correct "eh."

- Pay special attention to the editor's suggested dynamic and phrase markings. Consider how to make each repetition of a section unique and interesting. The repetition that makes "Viva Tutti" easy to learn also makes it difficult to sing musically. For example, try making mm. 13-17 more legato than the sections around it.

- Remind First Tenors to maintain a steady pitch when other voice parts change as in m. 13.

- Emphasize word stress so that all repeated eighth notes do not "carry the same weight." Suggest that singers circle the syllables which should be stressed and concentrate on emphasizing the unstressed syllables much less. The editor has marked suggestions (‾ and >) for stressed syllables throughout. Use the exercise in the Vocal Technique section of the teacher's edition to rehearse the accents of beats in the music.

- For performance, find the key that best fits the choir. Don't hesitate to raise or lower a selection to fit your needs. Tuning may improve in a different key.

- "Viva Tutti" is appropriate for a small or large ensemble.

Evaluation:

- Evaluate "Americanization" of Italian vowels by following the Evaluation section on the student page. (*NS* 7A, 7B)

- Record rehearsals of "Viva Tutti" and ask students to evaluate intonation, dynamic contrasts, and balance among the three parts. Record and analyze frequently to note growth and improvement. (*NS* 7A, 7B)

Extension:

- Suggest that interested students research other songs which may have been sung by men's glee clubs. Other songs in this text which might fall into the category of "college glee club songs" include "Aura Lee" and "Viva la Compagnie!"

- Suggest that students analyze the repetition of sections in "Viva Tutti" and then improvise (using C pentatonic Orff instruments) a composition using that same form. (*NS* 3B)

Viva Tutti

(Here's To Beauty)

This traditional song is a favorite of tenor-bass choirs. This arrangement features a more useful English text, although this editor prefers the Italian. For a helpful guide to Italian pronunciation, see SINGER'S ITALIAN by Evelina Colorni (Schirmer Books).

Traditional Glee
Edited by EMILY CROCKER

English Lyrics by EMILY CROCKER

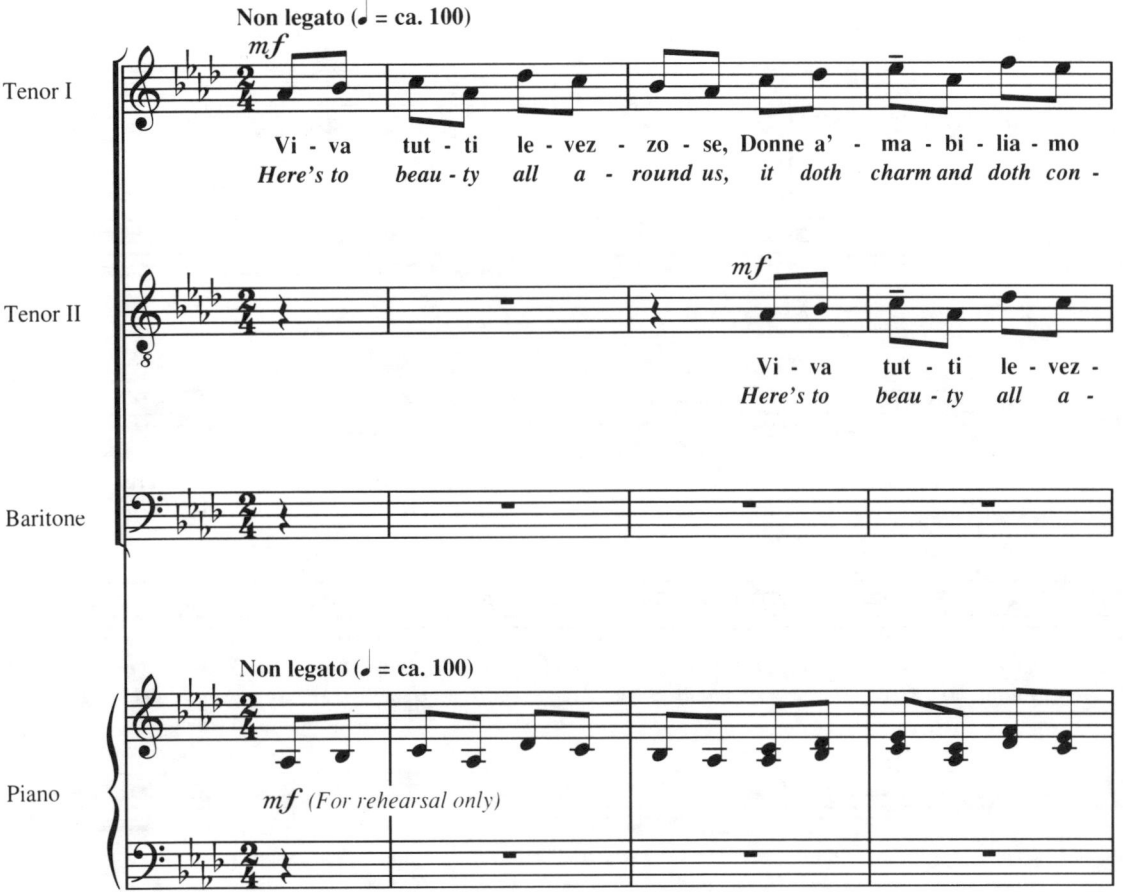

Student Book Page 145

Student Book Page 146

181

Student
Book Page
149

VIVE LA COMPAGNIE!

Composer: Traditional College
   Song, arranged by Ruth Artman
Text: Traditional
Voicing: TBB

Key: E♭ and E Major
Meter: 6/8
Form: A B A coda
Style: Arranged glee

Accompaniment: Piano
Programming: Concert or festival;
   good song to feature a men's
   chorus

Ranges:

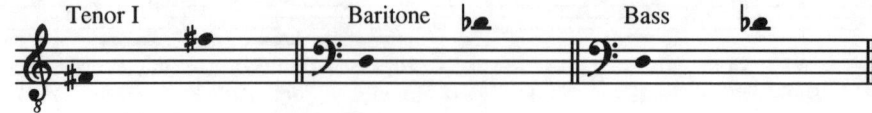

Student Book Page
150

VIVE LA COMPAGNIE!

Composer: Traditional College Song, arranged by Ruth Artman
Text: Traditional
Voicing: TBB

Cultural Context:
The contrasting 6/8 section and the *swing* section in this traditional college glee arrangement make it especially fun to sing. The word "glee" comes from the Anglo-Saxon word "gliw" meaning "entertainment." The first published collection of "glees" was in 1652, but they probably existed for many years before that. They were always intended to be fun and entertaining musical pieces.

French: *Vive l'amour*
Pronunciation: VEE-vuh lah-MOOR

            Vive la compagnie
            VEE-vuh lah kahm-pahn-NYEE

Musical Terms:
(♩ = 116)   *ff* (fortissimo)   *f* (forte)

unis. (unison)   > (accent)   (crescendo)

‾ (tenuto)   ⌢ fermata   // (caesura)

a tempo   ✗ (spoken)

Preparation:
Practice the two contrasting styles found in this music.

(m. 17 - "straight")

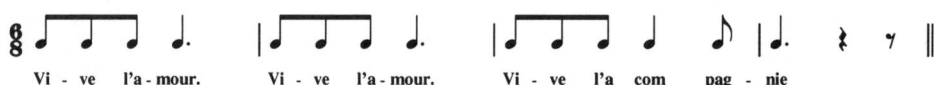

(m. 33 - "swing")

Evaluation:
Listen to an audio recording of your class performing this song. Evaluate the following:

• Did the choir sing the opening section with even eighth notes in a "straight" style?

• Did the choir sing the middle section in a "swing" style?

• Could you hear a contrast between the two sections of this song?

Objectives:

- The student will develop clear diction to convey the meaning of the text. (*National Standard* 1A)
- The singer will recognize, discuss, and perform music in ABA form. (*NS* 5D)

Historical/Stylistic Guidelines:

Originally a "glee" was a three-part a cappella piece sung by men. Large college organizations developed glee clubs in which men met and sang songs like "Vive La Compagnie!" Probably the most famous glee club was the Yale Glee Club. Glee club songs were usually not serious and were meant to be enjoyed by those singing them.

Ruth Artman, composer, arranger, conductor and teacher, began her serious compositional career customizing choral music for her students at the start of her teaching experience. She now has over 200 works in print. Mrs. Artman has taught music on all levels from kindergarten through graduate school, as well as being involved in church music. She has appeared professionally throughout the United States, Canada, and Europe, directing special choral groups, reading sessions, clinics, festivals, and workshops.

Vocal Technique/Warm-Ups/Exercises:

- Articulation and clarity of text is important to a successful performance of this song. Practice the lines printed below:

    Let ev'ry good fellow now join in the song!
    Success to each other and pass it along!

    If time or occasion compel us to part,
    These days shall forever enliven the heart.

    - in a whisper exaggerating the consonants.
    - spoken maintaining the same clarity and energy.
    - with exaggeration of movement in the mouth, lips, and tongue.

- Review the pronunciation guide as found in the Preparation section of the student page.

Rehearsal Guidelines and Notes
Suggested Sequence:

1. Familiarize students with the musical terms found in this piece as listed in the student text. (*NS* 5C)

2. Observe that mm. 55-68 is exactly the same as mm. 5-18 only raised a half step in pitch (A section). Teach these two sections first by having students:

    - chant the words in rhythm
    - add pitch to words one part at a time
    - combine parts

3. Next, teach the B section (mm. 21-52) using the sequence described above. Pay close attention to the rhythm.

4. Finally, teach the coda at m. 69.

5. As you practice the entire song, remind students to pay particular attention to the dynamics indicated in the score.

Performance Tips:

- In mm. 33-36, to show greater dynamic contrast and add excitement to the performance, begin much softer than the *mf* indicated in the score. Practice a gradual crescendo to the *fortissimo*.

- Stress all accented notes. Explode the consonants and go directly to the vowel sounds.

- In mm. 5-8 and each instance similar to it, sing the forte softer (*mp*) to create greater contrast with the *fortissimo* that follows.

- Because of the quick tempo in the A section, avoid clipping off the end of the phrases. Hold the last note of the phrase for full value. For example: "join in a song" m. 6; or "pass it a-long" m. 10.

- You may wish to use this song as a teaching tool to introduce 6/8 meter. Have students count or conduct the patterns from the song.

- This song is most effective when performed with energy and gusto.

Evaluation:

- Lead the class in completing the Evaluation section found on the student page. (*NS* 7A, 7B)

- Record a rehearsal performance and ask singers to analyze where dynamic contrasts could have been greater. Can the chorus sing *forte* or *fortissimo* and still keep a full, rich, in-tune sound?

Extension:

- Select a student to create choreography for this song. You may want to suggest adding straw hats and canes. Be creative!

- Suggest that students attempt to arrange a familiar song in "swing style" using the middle section of "Viva la Compagnie!" as a model. (*NS* 4B)

To The Clay Male Ensemble

Vive La Compagnie!

For TBB and Piano

Traditional
Arranged by RUTH ARTMAN

Student
Book Page
153

Sing vi - ve, vi - ve com - pag - nie!_____

(unis.)

Sing vi - ve, vi - ve com - pag - nie!_____

49

This is the song of vi - ve la com-pag - nie!_____

49

This is the song of vi - ve la com-pag - nie!_____

Slower (♩. =96)

55 Deliberately

_f_ If time or oc - ca - sion com-pel us to part,

If time shall com - pel us to part,

Slower (♩. =96)

55 Deliberately

191

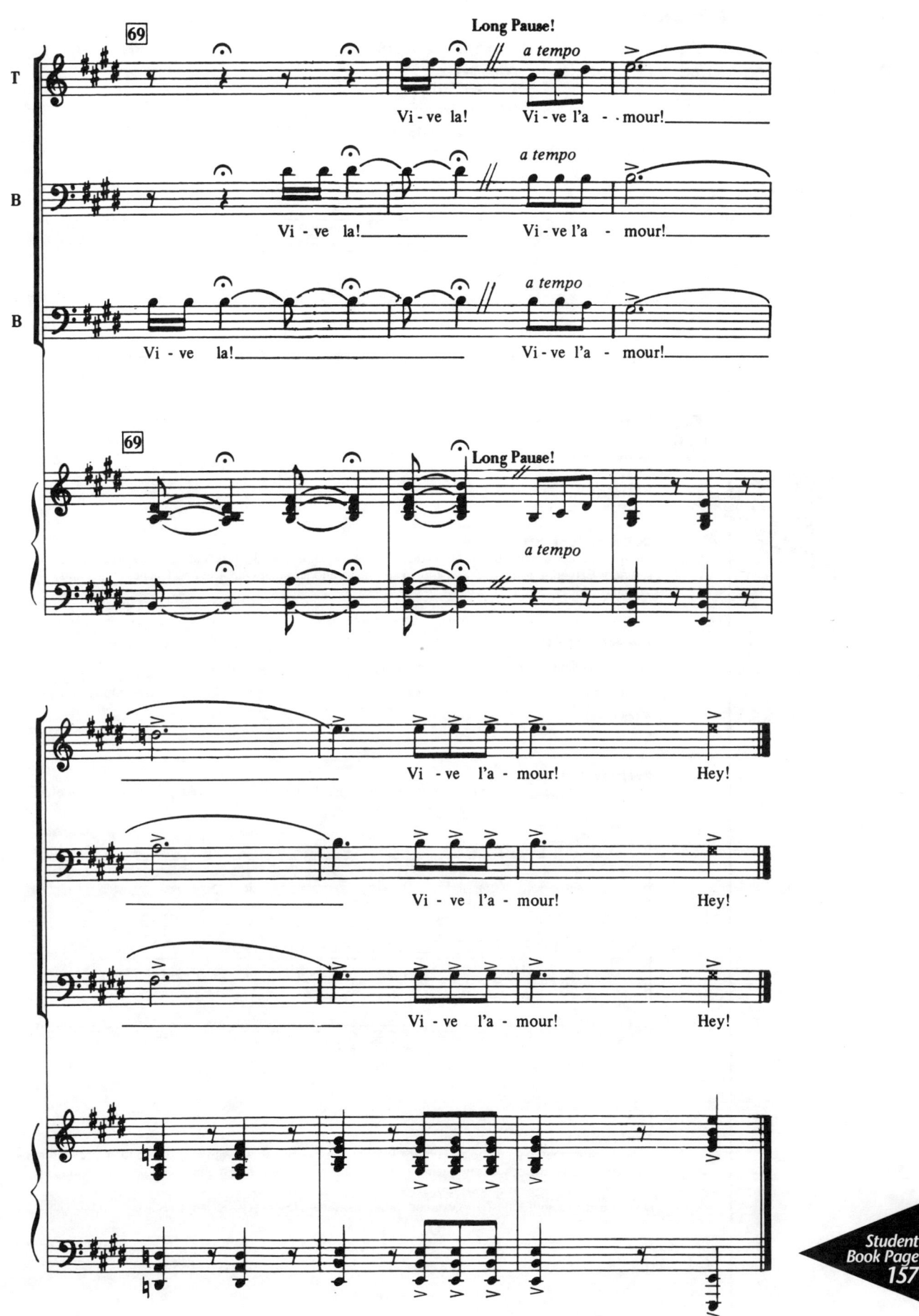

WHILE BY MY SHEEP

Composer: Traditional Carol,
    arranged by Catherine Bennett
Text: Traditional Carol
Voicing: TTB

Key: D♭/B♭ Major
Meter: 4/4
Form: Strophic
Style: Traditional holiday, sacred
Accompaniment: a cappella

Programming: Holiday concert

Ranges:

Student Book Page 158

WHILE BY MY SHEEP

Composer: Arranged by Catherine Bennett
Text: Traditional Carol
Voicing: TTB a cappella

Cultural Context:
This traditional carol tells of the shepherds tending their flocks on the first Christmas Eve. The arranger of this setting is Catherine Bennett, a well-known composer and arranger who lives and teaches in Olympia, Washington.

Musical Terms:

mp (mezzo piano)   *mf* (mezzo forte)   *p* (piano)

🎵 (fermata)   *cresc.* (crescendo)   _____ (crescendo)

// (caesura)   *a tempo*

Preparation:
The use of echo sections is found throughout this piece. Practice these lines with the dynamics indicated.

Evaluation:
Give each member of your choir a number. Practice the exercise above with only the "odd" numbered choir members singing the echoes and then with the "even" numbered choir members singing the echoes.

Does the echo sound softer? This exercise should demonstrate the echo feeling effectively.

194

Objectives:

- The student will perform dynamic and tempo changes as indicated by the composer or arranger. (*National Standard* 1E)
- The student will perform seasonal choral literature. (*NS* 1E)

Historical/Stylistic Guidelines:

"While By My Sheep" tells of the angels coming to the shepherds that were tending their flocks and announcing the birth of the Christ child in Bethlehem. It is based on the traditional German carol, "Als Ics Meinen Schafen Wacht," which was part of a sixteenth century nativity play. A shepherd sang the solo verses onstage and was answered in the echos by an offstage chorus.

This arrangement employs the musical concept of antiphonal singing. According to the *Oxford Dictionary of Music*, antiphonal singing is "when two parts of a choir sing alternatively, one answering the other."

Catherine Bennett arranged "While By My Sheep" for her own boys' choir. She has taught middle school choir and drama, and currently teaches humanities in Olympia, Washington.

Vocal Technique/Warm-Ups/Exercises:

Exercise 1:

In many instances, the male singer with a changing voice sings with a tone that is placed too far back in the throat. Practice this exercise daily concentrating on a forward tone.

- Ask the singers to maintain the "buzz" as long as possible on the Z and M.
- Repeat up by half steps.

Exercise 2:

There are many descending eighth note passages written in "While By My Sheep." Practice the following exercise and listen for clear, clean eighth note runs.

- Change the key of these exercises to fit the choir or section of the choir.

Rehearsal Guidelines and Notes
Suggested Sequence:

1. Familiarize students with the musical terms found in this piece as listed in the student text. (*NS* 5C)
2. Chant the rhythm to the first verse (mm. 1-12). Add the pitches. As this material is introduced, remind the singers of the importance of the softer dynamic level in each echo section.
3. Review the material found in the Preparation section of the student page.
4. Repeat the same procedure for the next verse (mm. 13-26). Note that both the rhythm and melodic patterns are very different from the first verse.

195

5. Before adding the last verse, go back and review the two verses already introduced and listen for a clear definition of parts. Reteach material if necessary. Check for understanding of the *rallantando* marking at m. 25.

6. Introduce the last verse (mm. 27-36). Point out that the basses now have the melody and the two tenor parts have the supplemental harmony. Note the *a tempo* marking.

7. Because of the changes in the melody and rhythm, teach the last three measures (mm. 37-39) as a separate lesson.

8. Remind the students to pay particular attention to the tempo markings and dynamics indicated in the score.

Performance Tips:

- It is essential that the choir observes the many dynamic changes indicated in the score.
- Remind the singers to use clear, crisp articulation when singing "While By My Sheep." Ask them to explode the consonants and go directly to a tall vowel sound.
- Strive for very tall vowel sounds on words like joy, high, the, while, and my. See *Essential Musicianship* - Book I student page 5 for more information on tall vowel sounds.
- Observe all of the crescendos and decrescendos in each line.
- All echo parts may be sung by a trio or small ensemble if desired.
- For performance, find the key that best fits the choir. Don't be afraid to raise or lower a selection to fit the choir's needs.

Evaluation:

- See the Evaluation section of the student page. (*NS 7A, 7B*)
- Select one or two singers from each section to come forward, listen critically, and report on the following: (*NS 7A, 7B*)

    - A difference in dynamic level in the echo sections
    - Clear, crisp diction
    - Definition of parts

For Karen Fulmer

While By My Sheep

For TBB a cappella

Traditional Carol
Arranged by CATHERINE BENNETT

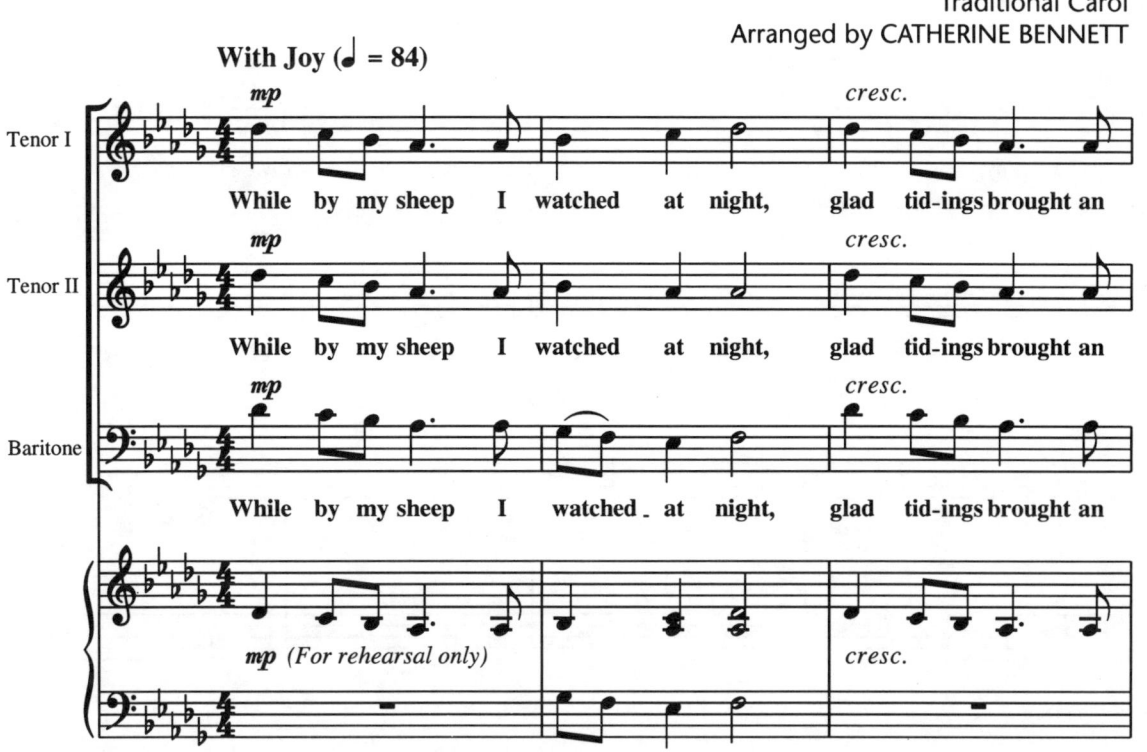

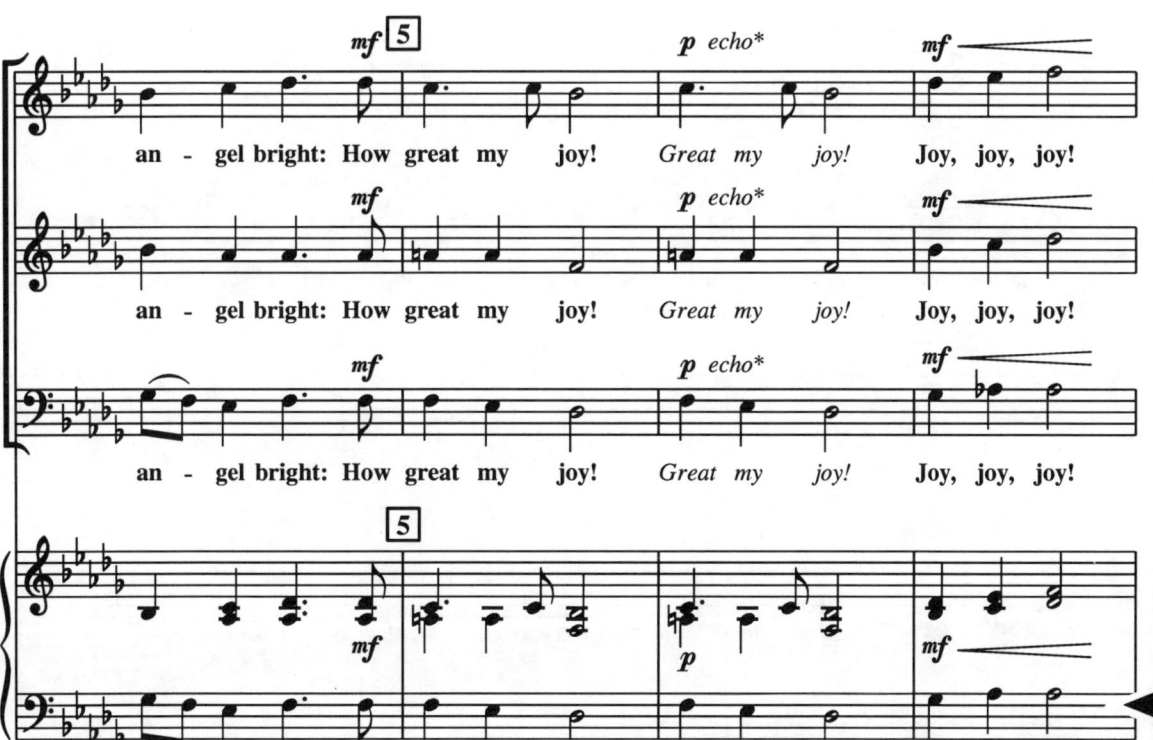

*All echo parts may be sung by a trio or a small group, if desired.

197

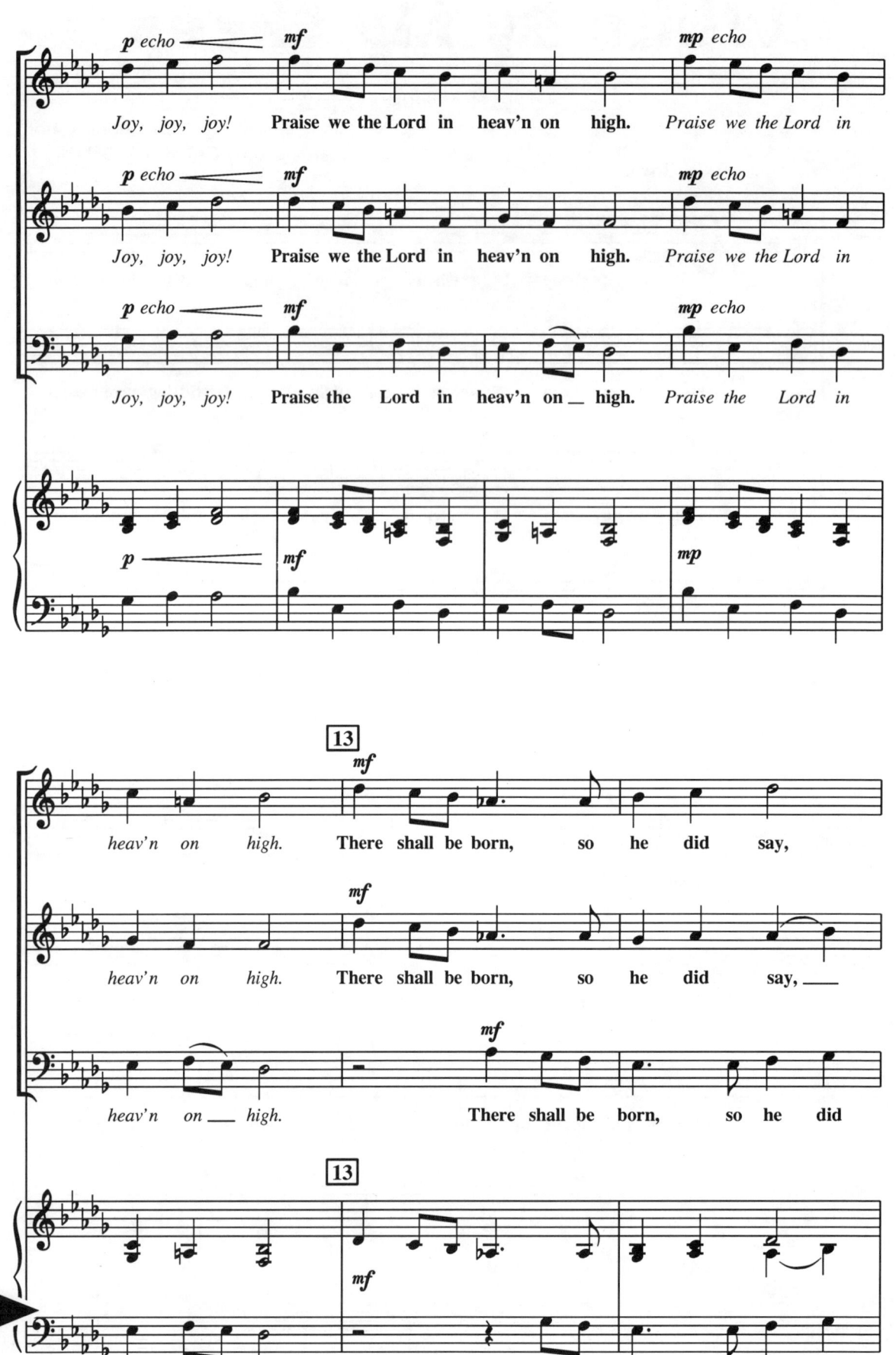

in Beth-le-hem, a child to-day. How great my joy!

in Beth-le-hem a child to-day. How great my joy! _____

say, in Beth-le-hem to-day. How great my joy! _____

p echo   *mf* _____   *mp echo*

Great my joy! Joy, joy, joy! Joy, joy, joy!

p echo   *mf* _____   *mp echo*

How great my joy! _____ Joy, joy, oh, joy! _ Joy, joy! _

p echo   *mf* _____   *mp echo*

How great my joy! _____ Joy, joy, oh, joy! _ Joy, joy! _

p   *mf* _____   *mp*

199

Praise we the Lord in heav'n on high. *Praise we the Lord in*

Praise we the Lord in heav'n on high. *Praise we the Lord in*

Praise we the Lord _ in __ heav'n_on __ high. ___ *Praise we the Lord _ in __*

heav'n on high. Praise the Lord _ on __ high!

heav'n on high. Praise the Lord_ the Lord on high!

heav'n _ on __ high. ___ Praise _ we the Lord on high! For

Student Book Page 162

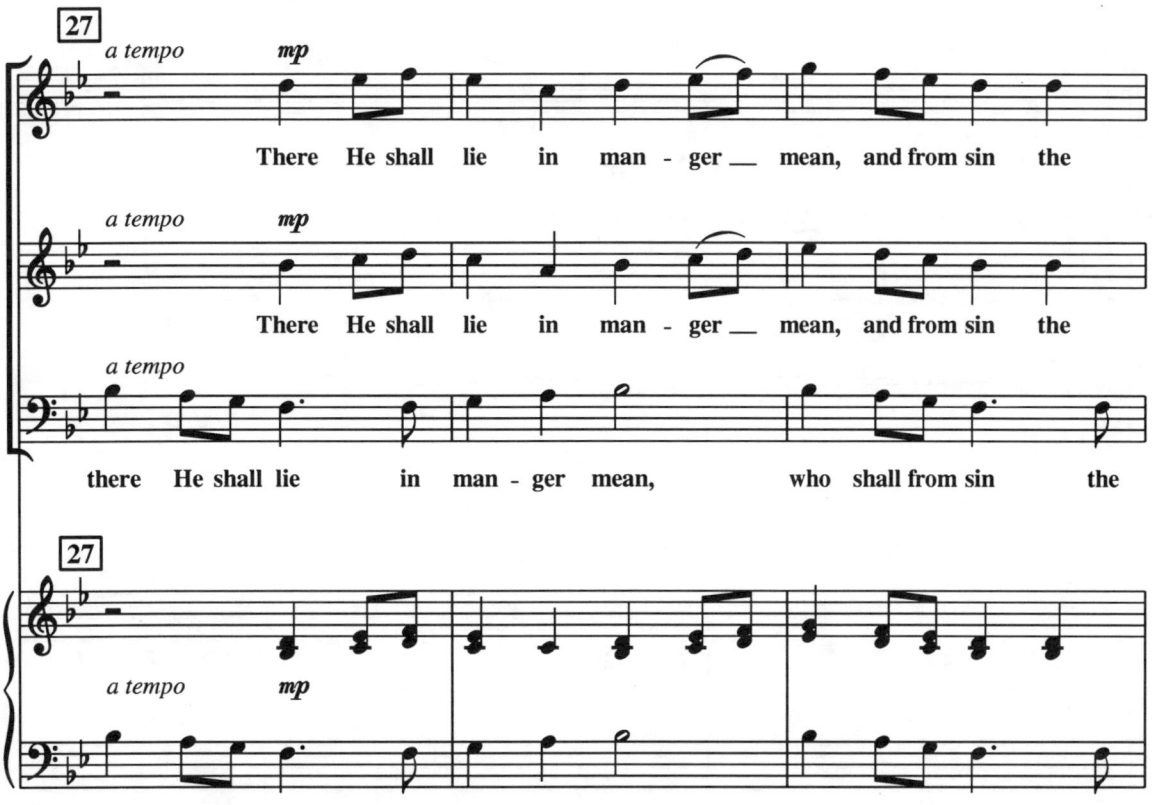

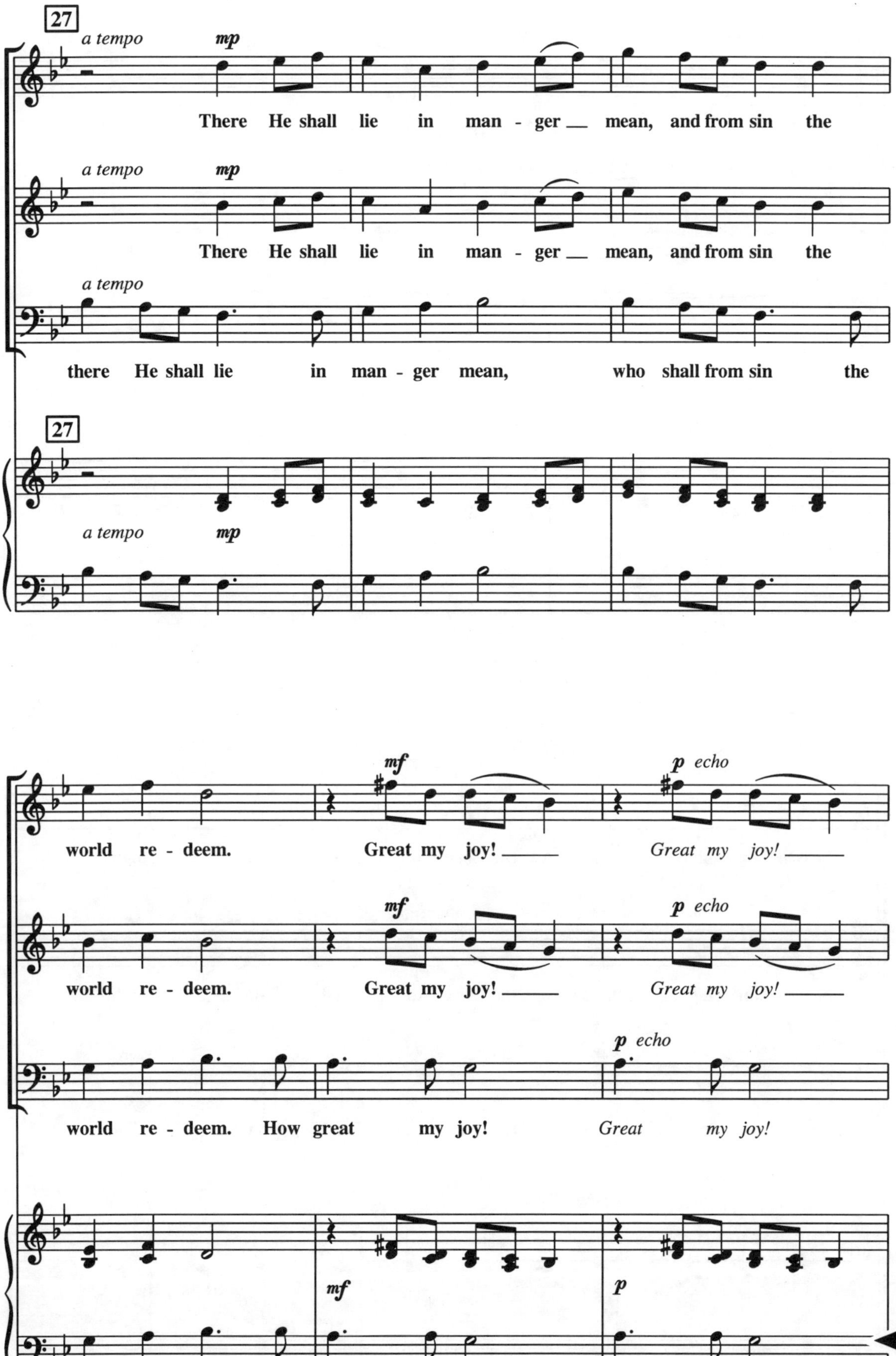
27
a tempo
mp
There He shall lie in man - ger mean, and from sin the
a tempo
mp
There He shall lie in man - ger mean, and from sin the
a tempo
there He shall lie in man - ger mean, who shall from sin the
27
a tempo
mp
mf
p echo
world re - deem. Great my joy!
Great my joy!
mf
p echo
world re - deem. Great my joy!
Great my joy!
p echo
world re - deem. How great my joy!
Great my joy!
mf
p

Student Book Page 163

Joy, joy, joy! _____ Joy, joy, joy! _____ Praise we the Lord in

Joy, joy, joy! _____ Joy, joy, joy! _____ Praise we the Lord in

Joy, joy, joy! _____ Joy, joy, joy! _____ Praise we the Lord in

heav'n on high. Praise we the Lord, the Lord on high!

heav'n on high. Praise we the Lord, the Lord on _____ high!

heav'n on high. Praise we the Lord, the Lord on high!

Student Book Page 164

 **GLOSSARY**

a cappella [It.] (ah-kah-PEH-lah) - Singing without instrumental accompaniment.

accelerando (*accel.*) [It.] (ahk-chel-leh-RAHN-doh) - Becoming faster; a gradual increase in tempo.

accent (>) - Stress or emphasize a note (or chord) over others around it. Accents occur by singing the note louder or stressing the beginning consonant or vowel.

accidentals - Symbols that move the pitch up or down a half step.
- sharp (♯) - raises the pitch one half step.
- flat (♭) - lowers the pitch one half step.
- natural (♮) - cancels a previous *sharp* or *flat*. (When it cancels a flat, the pitch is raised one half step; when it cancels a sharp, the pitch is lowered one half step).

Accidentals affect all notes of the same pitch that follow the accidental within the same measure, or if an altered note is *tied* over a *barline*.

adagio [It.] (ah-DAH-jee-oh) - Tempo marking indicating slow.

al fine [It.] (ahl FEE-neh) - To ending. An indicator following *D.C.* or *D.S.*. From the Latin *finis,* "to finish."

allargando (*allarg.*) [It.] (ahl-lar-GAHN-doh) - Broadening, becoming slower, sometimes with an accompanying *crescendo*.

allegro [It.] (ah-LEH-groh) - Tempo marking indicating fast.

alto - A treble voice that is lower than the *soprano*, usually written in the *treble clef*.

andante [It.] (ahn-DAHN-teh) - Tempo marking indicating medium or "walking" tempo.

animato [It.] (ah-nee-MAH-toh) - Style marking meaning animated.

arranger - The person who takes an already existing composition and reorganizes it to fit a new instrumentation or voicing.

articulation - The clear pronunciation of text using the lips, teeth, and tongue. The singer must attack consonants crisply and use proper vowel formation.

a tempo - Return to the original tempo.

balletto [It.] (bah-LEH-toh) - A 16th century vocal composition with dance-rhythms and often phrases of nonsense syllables like "fa-la-la." Giovanni Gastoldi wrote the earliest known collection of balletti.

bar - See *measure*.

barline - A vertical line that divides the staff into smaller sections called measures. A double barline indicates the end of a section or piece of music.

Barline   Double Barline

Baroque Period (ca. 1600-1750) - (bah-ROHK) The period in Western music history that extended from 1600 to about 1750; also the musical styles of that period. The style features of most Baroque music are frequent use of *polyphony*; fast, motor-like rhythms; and use of the chorale. Some famous Baroque composers were J.S. Bach, G.F. Handel, and Antonio Vivaldi.

bass - A male voice written in *bass clef* that is lower than a *tenor* voice.

bass clef - The symbol at the beginning of the staff used for lower voices and instruments, and the piano left hand. It generally refers to pitches lower the *middle C*. The two dots are on either side of F, so it is often referred to as the F clef.

beat - The unit of recurring pulse in music.

breath mark (❜) - An indicator within a phrase or melody where the musician should breathe. See also *no breath* and *phrase marking*.

caesura (//) [Fr.] (seh-SHOO-rah) - A break or pause between two musical phrases. Also called a *break*.

call and response - Alternation between two performers or groups of performers. Often used in *spirituals*, this technique begins with a leader (or group) singing a phrase followed by a response of the same phrase (or continuation of the phrase) by a second group.

canon - A musical form in which a melody in one part is followed a short time later by other parts performing the same melody. Canons are sometimes called *rounds*.

cantata [It.] (cahn-TAH-tah) - A large work (originally sacred) involving solos, chorus, organ, and occasionally orchestra. The cantata tells a story through text and music. Johann Sebastian Bach wrote a cantata for each Sunday of the church year.

chantey - A song sung by sailors in rhythm with their work.

chord - Three or more pitches sounding at the same time or in succession as in a broken chord. See also *interval*.

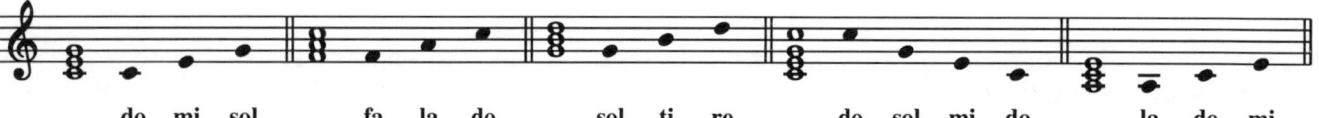

chromatic - Moving up or down by half steps, often outside of the key. Also the name of a scale composed entirely of half steps (all twelve pitches within an *octave*). The chromatic scale is distinct from the *diatonic* scale.

Classical Period (ca. 1750-1835) - The period in Western music history began in Italy in 1750 and continued until about 1825. Music of the Classical Period emphasized balance of phrase and structure. Ludwig von Beethoven, W.A. Mozart, and Joseph Haydn were famous composers from the Classical Period.

clef - The symbol at the beginning of the staff that identifies a set of pitches. See also *bass clef* and *treble clef*.

coda (⊕) [It.] (COH-dah) - Ending. A concluding portion of a composition.

common time (𝄴) - Another name for the meter 4/4. See also *cut time*.

composer - The writer or creator of a song or musical composition. See also *arranger*.

compound meter - Meters which have a multiple of 3 such as 6 or 9 (but not 3 itself). Compound meter reflects the note that receives the division unlike *simple meter*. (Ex. 6/8 = six divisions to the beat in two groups of three where the eighth note receives one division). An exception to the compound meter rule is when the music occurs at a slow tempo, then the music is felt in beats rather than divisions. See also *meter* and *time signature*.

con [It.] (kawn) - With.

crescendo (*cresc.* or ⟍⟍⟋⟋) [It.] (kreh-SHEN-doh) - Gradually growing louder. The opposite of *decrescendo*.

cued notes - Smaller notes indicating either *optional harmony* or notes from another voice part.

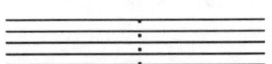

cut time (¢) - 2/2 time, the half note gets the beat.

da capo (D.C.) [It.] (dah KAH-poh) - Repeat from the beginning. See also *dal segno* and *al fine*.

dal segno (D.S.) [It.] (dahl SAYN-yoh) - Go back to the sign (𝄋) and repeat.

D.C. al fine [It.] - Repeat from the beginning to *fine* or end. See also *da capo* and *al fine*.

decrescendo (*decresc.* or ⟋⟋⟍⟍) [It.] (deh-kreh-SHEN-doh) - Gradually growing softer. The opposite of *crescendo*. See also *diminuendo*.

descant - A high ornamental voice part often lying above the melody.

diatonic - Step by step movement within a regular scale (any key). A combination of the seven whole and half steps (of different pitch names) in a key. Distinct from *chromatic*.

diminuendo (*dim.*) [It.] (dih-min-new-EN-doh) - Gradually growing softer. See also *decrescendo*.

diphthong (DIPH-thong) - A combination of two vowel sounds consisting of a primary vowel sound and a secondary vowel sound. The secondary vowel sound is (usually) at the very end of the diphthong. (Ex. The word "I" is really a diphthong using an "ah" and an "ee." The "ee" is a very brief sound at the end of the word.)

divisi (*div.*) [It.] (dee-VEE-see) - Divide; the parts divide.

dolce [It.] (DOHL-cheh) - Sweetly; usually soft as well.

dotted barline - A "helper" *barline* in songs with unusual *time signatures* such as 5/8 and 7/8. The dotted barline helps divide the measure into two or more divisions of *triple* or *duple* beat groups.

downbeat - The accented first beat of the measure.

D.S. al Coda [It.] (ahl KOH-dah) - Repeat from the sign (𝄋) and sing the *coda* when you see the symbol (⊕).

D.S. al fine [It.] (ahl FEE-neh) - Repeat from the sign (𝄋) to *fine* or ending.

duple - Any *time signature* or group of beats that is a multiple of 2.

dynamic - The loudness or softness of a line of music. Dynamic changes may occur frequently within a composition.

endings - ⌐1.‾‾‾ ⌐2.‾‾‾ (First and second endings) Alternate endings to a repeated section.

enharmonic - Identical tones which are named and written differently. For instance, F-sharp and G-flat are the same note, they are "enharmonic" with each other.

ensemble - A group of musicians, (instrumentalists, singers, or some combination) who perform together.

fermata (⌢) [It.] (fur-MAH-tah) - *or pause on* Hold the indicated note (or rest) for longer than its value; the length is left up to the interpretation of the director or the performer.

fine [It.] (FEE-neh) - Ending. From the Latin *finis*, "to finish." *Fr. Fini*

flat (♭) -An *accidental* that lowers the pitch of a note one half step. Flat also refers to faulty intonation when the notes are sung or played sightly under the correct pitch.

forte (*f*) [It.] (FOR-teh) - Loud.

fortissimo (*ff*) [It.] (for-TEE-see-moh) - Very loud.

freely - A style marking permitting liberties with tempo, dynamics, and style. *Rubato* may also be incorporated.

grand staff - A grouping of two staves.

half step - The smallest distance (or *interval*) between two notes on a keyboard. Shown symbolically (v). The *chromatic* scale is composed entirely of half steps.

half time - See *cut time.* ₵

harmonic interval - *Intervals* played simultaneously. *(within the regular scale?)*

harmony - Two or more musical tones sounding simultaneously.

hemiola [Gr.] (hee-mee-OH-lah) - A unique rhythmical device in which the beat of a *triple meter* has the feeling of *duple meter* (or the reverse) regardless of *barlines* and *time signatures*. This is accomplished through *ties* and/or *accent* placement.

homophony [Gr.] (haw-MAW-faw-nee) - Music in which melodic interest is concentrated in one voice part and may have subordinate accompaniment (distinct from *polyphony* in which all voice parts are equal). Homophony is also music which consists of two or more voice parts with similar or identical rhythms. From the Greek words meaning "same sounds," homophony could be described as being "hymn-style."

hushed - A style marking indicating a soft, whispered tone.

interval - The distance between two pitches.

intonation - Accuracy of pitch.

key - The organization of tonality around a single pitch (*key-note*). See also *key-note* and *key signature*.

key-note - The pitch which is the tonal center of a key. The first tone (note) of a scale. It is also called the *tonic*. A key is named after the key-note; for example in the key of A-flat, A-flat is the key-note. See also *key* and *key signature*.

key signature - The group of *sharps* or *flats* at the beginning of a staff which combine to indicate the locations of the key-note and configuration of the *scale*. If there are no sharps or flats, the key is automatically C major or A minor.

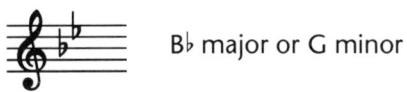 B♭ major or G minor

legato [It.] (leh-GAH-toh) - Smooth and connected. Opposite of *staccato*.

leadger lines (or leger lines) - The short lines used to extend the lines and spaces of the *staff*.

 *leger (It.) means light (lines.*

leggiero [It.] (leh-JEE-roh) - Light articulation; sometimes non-*legato*.

macaronic text - Text in which two languages are used (usually Latin and one other language).

madrigal - A kind of 16th century Italian composition based on secular poetry. Madrigals were popular into the 17th century.

maestoso [It.] (mah-ee-STOH-soh) - Majestic.

major key/scale/mode - A specific arrangement of whole steps and half steps in the following order:

Letter Names:	G	A	B	C	D	E	F♯	G
Moveable Do:	do	re	mi	fa	sol	la	ti	do
Fixed Do:	sol	la	ti	do	re	mi	fa	sol
Numbers:	1	2	3	4	5	6	7	1

See also *minor key/scale/mode.*

mass - The central religious service of the Roman Catholic Church. It consists of several sections divided into two groups: Proper of the Mass (text changes for every day) and Ordinary of the Mass (text stays the same in every mass). Between the years 1400 and 1600 the mass assumed its present form consisting of the Kyrie, Gloria, Credo, Sanctus, and Agnus Dei. It may include chants, hymns, and psalms as well. The mass also developed into large musical works for chorus, soloists, and even orchestra.

measure - A group of beats divided by *barlines*. Measures are sometimes called *bars*. The first beat of each measure is usually accented.

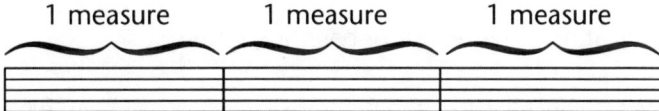

melisma - Long groups of notes sung on one syllable of text.

al - le - lu - ia

melodic interval - Notes that comprise an *interval* played in succession.

melody - A succession of musical tones; also the predominant line in a song.

meter - A form of rhythmic organization (grouping of beats). The kind of meter of designated by the *time signature*. See also *simple* and *compound meters*.

meter signature - See *time signature*.

metronome marking - A marking which appears over the top staff of music which indicates the kind of note which will get the beat, and the number of beats per minute as measured by a metronome. It reveals the *tempo*. (Ex. (♩ = 100)).

mezzo forte (*mf*) [It.] (MEH-tsoh FOR-teh) - Medium loud. *½ way between p & f*

mezzo piano (*mp*) [It.] (MEH-tsoh pee-AH-noh) - Medium soft. *½ way between p & f (also ?)*

middle C - The C which is located closest to the middle of the piano keyboard. Middle C can be written in either the *treble* or *bass clef*.

minor key/scale/mode - A specific arrangement of whole steps and half steps in the following order:

Letter Names:	D	E	F	G	A	B♭	C	D
Moveable Do:	la	ti	do	re	mi	fa	sol	la
Fixed Do:	re	mi	fa	sol	la	ti	do	re
Numbers:	6	7	1	2	3	4	5	6

See also *major key/scale/mode*.

mixed meter - Frequently changing meters or *time signatures* within a piece of music.

modulation - Changing keys within a song. Adjust to the *key signature*, the *key-note*, and proceed.

molto [It.] (MOHL-toh) - Much, very. (Ex. molto rit. = greatly slowing).

monophony - Music which consists of a single melody. This earliest form of composition is from the Greek words meaning "one sound." Chant or plainsong is monophony.

mysterioso [It.] (mih-steer-ee-OH-soh) - A style marking indicating a mysterious or haunting mood.

natural (♮) - Cancels a previous *sharp* (♯) or *flat* (♭). (When it cancels a flat, the pitch is raised one half step; when it cancels a sharp, the pitch is lowered one half step.)

no breath (◠ ◠ or N.B.) - An indication by either the *composer/arranger* or the editor of where *not* to breathe in a line of music. See also *phrase marking*.

notation - All written notes and symbols which are used to represent music.

octave - The *interval* between two notes of the same name. Octaves can be indicated within a score using 8*va* (octave above) and 8*vb* (octave below).

[handwritten: the TENOR G-Cleff is written with a figure 8 indicate it sounds on octave below & the treble G-cleff.]

ostinato [It.] (ah-stee-NAH-toh) - A repeated pattern used as a harmonic basis.

optional divisi (opt. div.) [It.] (dee-VEE-see) - The part splits into optional harmony. The smaller sized *cued notes* indicate the optional notes to be used.

phrase marking (⌢) - An indication by either the *composer* or the *arranger* as to the length of a line of music or melody. This marking often means that the musician is not to breathe during its duration. See also *no breath*.

piano (*p*) [It.] (pee-AH-noh) - Soft.

pianissimo (*pp*) [It.] (pee-ah-NEE-see-moh) - Very soft.

pick-up - An incomplete measure at the beginning of a song or phrase. *[handwritten: anacrusis(es) or lead-in]*

pitch - The highness or lowness of musical sounds. *[handwritten: frequency ~ etc... (comp. amplitude)]*

più [It.] (pew) - More. (Ex. più forte or più mosso allegro).

poco [It.] (POH-koh) - Little. (Ex. poco cresc. = a little crescendo).

poco a poco [It.] (POH-koh ah POH-koh) - Little by little (Ex. poco a poco cresc. = increase in volume, little by little).

polyphony [Gr.] (pahw-LIH-fahw-nee) - Music which consist of two or more independent melodies which combine to create simultaneous voice parts with different rhythms. Polyphony often involves contrasting dynamics and imitation from part to part. From the Greek words meaning "many sounds," polyphony is sometimes called counterpoint.

presto [It.] (PREH-stoh) - Very fast.

rallentando (*rall.*) [It.] (rahl-en-TAHN-doh) - Gradually slower. See also *ritardando*.

relative major/minor - Major and minor tonalities which share the same *key signature*.

[handwritten: (the Ecclesiatics refer to this period as the reformation)]

Renaissance Period (ca. 1450-1600) (REHN-neh-sahns) - A period in the Western world following the Middle Ages. Renaissance means "rebirth" and was a celebration of entrance into the modern age of thought and invention. In music it was a period of great advancement in notation and compositional ideas. *Polyphony* was developing and the *madrigal* became popular. Orlando di Lasso, Giovanni da Palestrina, Tomás Luis de Victoria, and Josquin Deprez were some of the more famous Renaissance composers.

repeat sign (||: :||) - Repeat the section. If the repeat sign is omitted, go back to the beginning. See also *endings*.

resolution (res.) - A progression from a dissonant tone or harmony to a consonant harmony. (Usually approached by step.) See also *suspension*.

rhythm - The organization of non-pitched sounds in time. Rhythm encompasses note and rest duration as well as *meters*, *tempos*, and their relationships.

ritardando (*rit.*) [It.] (ree-tahr-DAHN-doh) - Gradually slower. See also *rallentando*.

Romantic Period (ca. 1825-1900) - A period in 19th century Western art, literature, and music that lasted into the early 20th century. In music, as well as the other areas, Romanticism focused on the emotion of art. Works from this period emphasized the emotional effect music has on the listener through dynamic contrasts and different ways of changing the "mood." Opera flourished as well as chamber music. Some famous Romantic compsers are Franz Schubert, Frederick Chopin, Hector Berlioz, Johannes Brahms, and Richard Wagner. *to name but a few*

root/tone - The lowest note of a *triad* in its original position; the note on which the chord is built and named.

round - see *canon*.

rubato [It.] (roo-BAH-toh) - The tempo is free, left up to the interpretation of the director or performer.

scale - An inventory or collection of pitches. The word "scale" (from the Italian *scala*) means ladder. Thus, many musical scales are a succession of pitches higher and lower.

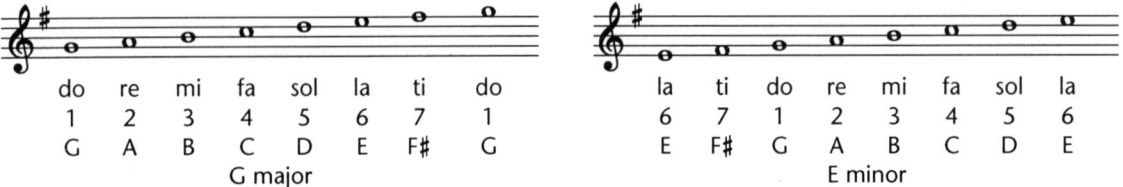

do	re	mi	fa	sol	la	ti	do
1	2	3	4	5	6	7	1
G	A	B	C	D	E	F#	G

G major

la	ti	do	re	mi	fa	sol	la
6	7	1	2	3	4	5	6
E	F#	G	A	B	C	D	E

E minor

score - The arrangement of a group of vocal and instrumental staffs which all sound at the same time.

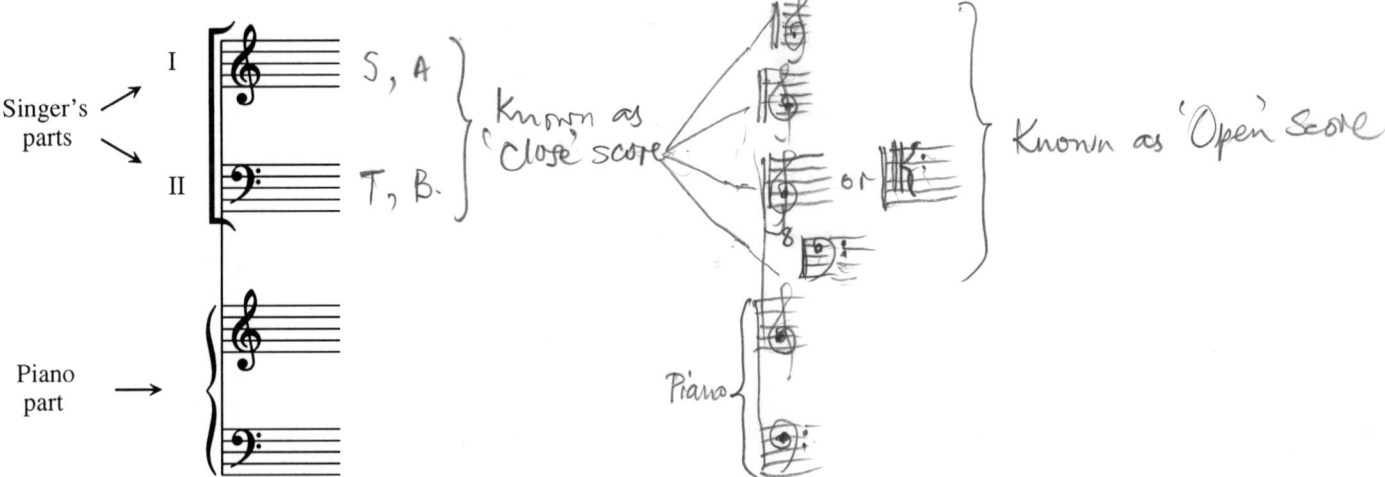

Singer's parts — I: S, A / II: T, B — Known as 'Close' score

Piano part — Known as 'Open' Score — Piano

sempre [It.] (SEHM-preh) - Always / continually. (Ex. sempre forte = always loud)

sequence - The successive repetition of a short melodic idea at different pitch levels.

sequence

sharp (#) - An *accidental* that raises the pitch of a note one half step. Also, faulty intonation in which the note is sung slightly above the correct pitch.

sign (𝄋 or Segno) [It.] (SAYN-yoh) - A symbol that marks the place in music where the musician is to skip back to from the *dal Segno (D.S.)*.

simile (*sim.*) [It.] - (SIM-eh-lee) Continue the same way. */similar way.*

simple meter - Meters which are based upon the note which receives the beat. (Ex. 4/4 or 𝄴 is based upon the quarter note receiving the beat.)

skip - The melodic movement of one note to another in *intervals* larger than a step.

slide (/♪) - To approach a note from underneath the designated pitch and "slide" up to the correct pitch. Slides often appear in jazz, pop tunes, and *spirituals*. *also in opera & orchestral "portemento"*

slur (♪ ♪) - A curved line placed above or below a group of notes to indicate that they are to be sung on the same text syllable. Slurs are also used in instrumental music to indicate that the group of notes should be performed *legato* (smoothly connected). *as a phrase. also referred to as a phrase-mark*

solfège [Fr.] (SOHL-fehj) - The study of sight-singing using pitch syllables (do re mi, etc.). *Tonic-Solfa*

soprano - The highest treble voice, usually written in *treble clef.*

spirito [It.] (SPEE-ree-toh) *with* / Spirit.

spiritual - Religious folk songs of African American origin associated with work, recreation, or religious gatherings. They developed prior to the Civil War and are still influential today. They have a strong rhythmic character and are often structured in *call and response.*

spoken - Reciting text with the speaking voice rather than singing the designated line. Often indicated with ⌐ instead of notes.

staccato (♪̇) [It.] (stah-KAH-toh -) Short, separated notes. Opposite of *legato.*

staff - The five horizontal parallel lines and four spaces between them on which notes are placed to show *pitch.*

```
5
4               4
3          3
2       2
1    1
```

The lines and spaces are numbered from the bottom up.

step - Melodic movement from one note to the next higher or lower *scale* degree.

style marking - An indicator at the beginning of a song or section of song which tells the musician in general what style the music should be performed. (Ex. *freely* or *animato*)

subito (*sub.*) [It.] (SOO-bee-toh) - Suddenly. (Ex. sub. piano = suddenly soft)

suspension (sus.) - The sustaining or "suspending" of a pitch from a consonant chord into a dissonant chord often using a *tie*. The resulting dissonant chord then *resolves* to a consonant chord. The musical effect is one of tension and release. See also *resolution.*

swing - A change in interpretation of eighth-note durations in some music (often jazz and blues). Groups of two eighth notes (♫) are no longer sung evenly, instead they are performed like part of a *triplet* (𝅘𝅥 ♪). The eighth-notes still appear ♫. A swing style is usually indicated at the beginning of a song or section. (♫ = 𝅘𝅥 ♪).

This was also used in Baroque period music in dance pieces and are used in interpretations of BACH, HANDEL style .etc...

211

syllables - Names given to pitch units or rhythm units to aid in sight-reading.

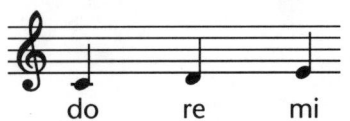

do   re   mi

ta   ta   ti ti   ta
1   2   3 &   4

syncopation - The use of *accents* and *ties* to create rhythmic interest. The result is a rhythmic pattern which stresses notes on the off beat. This technique is commonly found in *spirituals and jazz*. *classical, romantic and modern music*

tempo - The speed of the beat. *reference to Metronome markings*

tempo I - Return to the first tempo. Also called tempo primo. *or à tempo*

tenor - A male voice written in *bass clef* or *treble clef*. It is lower than the *alto*, but higher than the *bass*.

tenuto ( ) [It.] (teh-NOO-toh) - A slight stress on the indicated note. The note is held for its full value.

texture - The interrelationship of the voices and/or instruments within a piece of music. *Monophonic, homophonic,* and *polyphonic* are all types of textures. *chordal, block-chordal contrapuntal*

tie ( ) - A line connecting two or more notes of the same pitch so that their durations are their combined sum. Often occurring over *barlines*.

time signature - The symbol placed at the beginning of a composition or section to indicate its meter. This most often takes the form of a fraction (4/4 or 3/4), but may also involve a symbol as in the case of common time (C) and cut time (¢). The upper number indicates the number of beats in a measure and the lower number indicates which type of note recieving the beat. (An exception occurs in *compound meters*. See *compound meter* for an explanation.)

N.B. Time Signature are not written as fractions but one number over another. Check it out.

to coda - Go to the ⊕. *Usually a sign indicating a skip to ⊕ Coda.*

tonality - The organization of *pitches* in a song in which a certain pitch (tone) is designated as the *key-note* or the note which is the tonal center of a *key*. *i.e maj, minor, modal pentatonic, chromatic, blues wholetone, hungarian, oriental etc. (atonal)*

tone - A musical sound of definite pitch and quality.

tonic - The *key-note* of a key or scale.

tonic chord - The name given to the chord built on the *key-note* of the scale.

transpose - To rewrite or perform a song in a *key* other than the original. *transposing instruments Bb Eb F A*

treble clef - The symbol at the beginning of the staff used for higher voices and instruments, and the piano right hand. It generally refers to pitches higher then *middle* C. The curve is wrapped around the G, as a result it is also called the G clef. *But this G-Clef written with sub-script fig. 8 indicates a transpose —down an octave*

triad - A special type of 3-note chord built in 3rds over a *root tone*.

a musical decoration

trill (*tr* 〰) - Rapid alteration (within a key) between the marked note and the one above it.

triple *-time* / Any *time signature* or group of beats that is a multiple of 3.

triplet - A borrowed division of the beat where three notes of equal duration are to be sung/ *or played* in the time normally occupied by two notes of equal duration. Usually indicated with a 3.

unison (unis.) - All parts singing the same notes at the same time, (or singing in *octaves*).

villancico [Sp.] (vee-yahn-SEE-koh or bee-yahn-SEE-koh) - A composition of Spanish origin from the 15th and 16th centuries. Similar to the *madrigal,* this type of work is based on secular poetry and is structured around the verses and refrains of its text. *In Spanish v ≡ b are very similar equivalent sounds*

vivace [It.] (vee-VAH-cheh) - Very fast.

whole step - The combination of two successive half steps. Shown symbolically (ᴜ). *presumably ½ step (ᴠ)?*

BIBLIOGRAPHY

Alderson, Richard. *Complete Handbook of Voice Training*. West Nyack, New York: Parker Publishing Co., Inc., 1979.

Baker, Theodore, ed. *Schirmer Pronouncing Pocket Manual of Musical Terms*. 4th ed., rev. by Nicolas Slonimsky. New York: Schirmer Books, 1978.

___. *Baker's Biographical Dictionary of Musicians*. 6th ed., completely rev. by Nicolas Slonimsky. New York: Schirmer Books, 1978.

Bartle, Jean A. *Lifeline for Children's Choir Directors*. London: Oxford Press, 1988.

Bjorneberg, Paul, ed. *Exploring Careers in Music*. Reston, Virginia: Music Educators National Conference, 1990.

Claghorn, Charles Eugene. *Biographical Dictionary of American Music*. West Nyack, New York: Parker Publishing, Co., 1973.

Coffin, Berton. *Overtones of Bel Canto*. Metuchen, New Jersey: The Scarecrow Press, 1980.

Collins, Don L. *Teaching Choral Music*. Englewood Cliffs, New Jersey: Prentice-Hall, 1993.

Consortium of National Arts Education Associations. *National Standards for Arts Education: What Every Young American Should Know and Be Able to Do in the Arts*. Reston, Virginia: Music Educators National Conference, 1994.

Cooksey, John M. "The Development of a Contemporary, Eclectic Theory for the Training and Cultivation of the Junior High School Male Changing Voice." Parts 1-4. *Choral Journal* 18:2-5 (1977-78). (Note: These are four articles printed in a series.)

Decker, Harold A., and Julius Herford, eds. *Choral Conducting Symposium*. 2nd ed. Englewood Cliffs, New Jersey: Prentice Hall, Inc., 1988.

De Angelis, Michael. *The Correct Pronunciation of Latin According to Roman Usage*. St. Gregory Guild, Inc., 1965.

Downs, Philip G. *Classical Music: The Era of Haydn, Mozart, and Beethoven*. New York: W.W. Norton & Company, Inc., 1992.

Ehmann, Wilhelm, and Frauke Haasemann. *Voice Building for Choirs*. Chapel Hill, North Carolina: Hinshaw Music, Inc., 1982.

Ehret, Walter, and George K. Evans. *The International Book of Christmas Carols*. Englewood Cliffs, New Jersey: Prentice-Hall, 1963.

Ewen, David. *All the Years of American Popular Music*. Englewood Cliffs, New Jersey: Prentice-Hall, Inc., 1977.

___. *The Complete Book of Classical Music*. Englewood Cliffs, New Jersey: Prentice-Hall, Inc., 1966.

___. *The World of Twentieth Century Music*. Englewood Cliffs, New Jersey: Prentice-Hall, Inc., 1968.

Feitz, Leland. *Cripple Creek! A Quick History of the World's Greatest Gold Camp*. Colorado Springs, Colorado: Little London Press, 1967.

Gackle, Lynn. "The Adolescent Female Voice: Characteristics of Change and Stages of Development." *Choral Journal* 31(8)(1991): 17-25.

Grout, Donald J., and Claude V. Palisca. *A History of Western Music*. 4th ed. New York: W.W. Norton & Company, Inc., 1988.

Grun, Bernard. *The Timetables of History*. 3rd ed. New York: Simon & Schuster, 1991.

Haasemann, Frauke, and James M. Jordan. *Group Vocal Techniques*. Chapel Hill, North Carolina: Hinshaw Music Inc. 1991.

Hoffer, Charles R. *Teaching Music in the Secondary Schools*. 4th ed. Belmont, California: Wadsworth Publishing, Company, 1991.

Johnston, Richard. *Folk Songs North America Sings*. Toronto: E. C. Kerby, Ltd., 1984.

Kennedy, Michael. *The Concise Oxford Dictionary of Music.* 3rd ed. Oxford, England: Oxford University Press, 1980.

Lamb, Gordon H. *Choral Techniques.* 3rd ed. Dubuque, Iowa: Wm. C. Brown Company Publishers, 1988.

Lomax, Alan. *The Folk Songs of North America.* Garden City, New York: Doubleday & Company, Inc., 1975.

Marshall, Madeleine. *The Singer's Manual of English Diction.* New York: Schirmer Books, 1953.

May, Wiliiam V., and Craig Tolin. *Pronunciation Guide for Choral Literature: French, German, Hebrew, Italian, Latin, Spanish.* Reston, Virginia: Music Educators National Conference, 1987.

Music Educators National Conference, Committee on Standards. *Guidelines for Performances of School Music Groups: Expectiations and Limitations.* Reston, Virginia: Music Educators National Conference, 1986.

Music Educators National Conference, Task Force on Choral Music Course of Study. *Teaching Choral Music: A Course of Study.* Reston, Virginia: Music Educators National Conference, 1991.

Morgan, Robert P. *Twentieth-Century Music: A History of Musical Style in Modern Europe and America.* New York: W.W. Norton & Company, Inc., 1991.

New York State School Music Association. *NYSSMA Manual: A Resource Manual of Graded Solo & Ensemble Music, Suitable for Contests and Festivals.* Westbury, New York: New York State School Music Association, 1991.

Palisca, Claude V., ed. *Norton Anthology of Western Music, Vol. I.* New York: W. W. Norton & Company, 1980.

Pfautsch, Lloyd. *English Diction for Singers.* New York: Lawson Gould, Inc., 1971.

Plantiga, Leon. *Romantic Music: A History of Musical Style in Nineteenth-Century Europe.* New York: W.W. Norton & Company, Inc., 1984.

Randel, Don M., ed. *The New Harvard Dictionary of Music.* Cambridge, Massachusetts: The Belknap Press of Harvard University Press, 1986.

Rao, Doreen. *We Will Sing: Choral Music Experience.* New York: Boosey & Hawkes, 1993.

___, ed. *Choral Music for Children: An Annotated List.* Reston, Virginia: Music Educators National Conference, 1990.

Robinson, Ray and Allen Winold. *The Choral Experience.* New York: Harper's College Press, 1976.

Roe, Paul F. *Choral Music Education.* 2nd ed. Englewood Cliffs, New Jersey: Prentice-Hall, Inc., 1983.

Runfola, Maria, ed. *Proceedings of the Symposium on the Male Adolescent Changing Voice.* Buffalo, New York: State University of New York at Buffalo Press, 1984.

Sandburg, Carl. *The American Songbag.* New York: Harcourt Brace Jovanovich, Inc., 1955.

Sadie, Stanley, ed. *The New Grove Dictionary of Music and Musicians.* Washington D.C.: Grove's Dictionaries of Music, 1980.

Shaw, Kirby. *Vocal Jazz Style.* 2nd ed. Milwaukee, Wisconsin: Hal Leonard Corporation, 1987.

Stanton, Royal. *Steps to Singing for Voice Classes.* 2nd ed. Belmont, California: Wadsworth Publishing Company, Inc., 1976.

Ulrich, Homer. *A Survey of Choral Music.* New York: Harcourt Brace Jovanovich, Inc., 1973.

University Interscholastic League. *Prescribed Music List for Bands, Orchestras and Choirs.* University Interscholastic League, 1991-1994.

Uris, Dorothy. *To Sing in English.* New York: Boosey and Hawkes, 1971.

Vennard, William. *Singing, the Mechanism and the Technique.* New York: Carl Fischer, 1988.

Wall, Joan Robert Caldwell, Tracy Gavilanes, and Sheila Allen. *Diction for Singers: A Concise Reference for English, Italian, Latin, German, French, and Spanish Pronunciation.* Dallas: PST... Inc., 1990.

Young, Carlton R. *Companion to the United Methodist Hymnal.* Nashvillle, Tennessee: Abingdon Press, 1993.

RECOMMENDED VIDEOS

Archibeque, Charlene, *Daily Workout for a Beautiful Voice: Featuring Charlotte Adams.* Santa Barbara, California: Santa Barbara Music Publishing.

Ehly, Eph. *Choral Singing Style.* Milwaukee, Wisconsin: Hal Leonard Corporation.

___. *Excellence in Conducting "The Natural Approach."* Milwaukee, Wisconsin: Hal Leonard Corporation.

___. *Positive Motivation for the Choral Rehearsal.* Milwaukee, Wisconsin: Hal Leonard Corporation.

___. *Tuning the Choir.* Milwaukee, Wisconsin: Hal Leonard Corporation.

Hassemann, Frauke, and James Jordan. *Group Vocal Technique.* Chapel Hill, North Carolina: Hinshaw Music.

Jacobson, John. *John Jacobson's Riser Choreography.* Milwaukee, Wisconsin: Hal Leonard Corporation.

Nelson, Charles, Austin King, and Jon Ashby. *The Voice: Three Professionals Discuss the Function, Abuses and Care of the Most Important Instrument of Communication.* Abilene, Texas: Voice Institute of West Texas at Abilene Christian University.

Wall, Joan, and Robert Caldwell. *The Singer's Voice: Breath.* Dallas, Texas: Pst...Inc.

___. *The Singer's Voice: Vocal Folds.* Dallas, Texas: Pst...Inc.

___. *The Singer's Voice: Vocal Tract.* Dallas, Texas: Pst...Inc.

___. *The Singer's Voice: Acoustics.* Dallas, Texas: Pst...Inc.

ABOUT THE AUTHORS

JANICE KILLIAN is a South Dakota native and a Texan by marriage. Her undergraduate studies include work at Augustana College in Sioux Falls, South Dakota, and a degree in music education from the University of Kansas. Her graduate work includes a masters at the University of Connecticut and a Ph.D. in music education from the Univeristy of Texas-Austin.

Dr. Killian has taught at every level. Since 1968, her teaching career has included K-12 choral music in Bladwin City, Kansas; middle school general music in East Hartford, Connecticut; choral director grades 7-12 in suburban Minneapolis (Edina, Minnesota); member of the music education faculty at the State University of New York in Buffalo; choral/general specialist in grades 7-8 in Austin, Texas; and junior high choral director in suburban Dallas (Carrollton-Farmers Branch Independent School District). Dr. Killian's choirs are frequent sweepstakes winners and she is known as a master teacher, having received teaching awards at each level in which she has taught.

In 1990 Dr. Killian joined the faculty at Texas Woman's University in Denton, Texas, where her duties include directing a choral ensemble, teaching graduate and undergraduate music education classes, supervising student teachers, and conducting music education research.

Dr. Killian is an active researcher whose studies appear frequently in national journals. Her research interests have focused primarily on the junior high choral experience, changing voices, and preference research relative to junior high singers. She is a member of the editorial board for the *Journal of Research in Music Education*. She is a frequent choral clinician and adjudicator, and conducts workshops on the topic of assessment in the arts. Dr. Killian is actively involved in state and national music education organizations.

MICHAEL O'HERN has been the choral director at Lake Highlands Junior High in Richardson, Texas, since the fall of 1982. A graduate of West Texas State Univeristy, Mr. O'Hern has completed graduate work at East Texas State University and the University of Texas at Arlington.

He has served as Texas Region III Junior High Vocal Chairman and as a clinician and adjudicator throughout the state. In 1984, Mr. O'Hern was chosen as an Oustanding Young Man of America and in 1987 he was awarded the Texas PTA Honorary Lifetime Membership. He was chosen as a 1988 RISE Foundation "Teacher of the Year" for the Richardson Independent School District. Mr. O'Hern has served on the state vocal committee for the 1995-1998 Texas Prescribed Music List.

While at Lake Highlands, Mr. O'Hern's choirs have been consistent sweepstakes winners at University Interscholastic League Competition. His choirs have won the Six Flags Over Texas Contest and the Adjudicators National Invitational Festival in Washington, D.C.. The Lake Highlands Chorale performed for the Texas Music Educators convention in 1989 and 1994.

Mr. O'Hern performed in the *Texas* outdoor musical drama in Canyon, Texas, for four years and serves as a soloist throughout the Dallas area. His professional affiliations include membership in the Richardson Education Association, Texas Music Educators Association, Texas Choral Directors Association, Texas Music Adjudicators Association, and American Choral Directors Association.

LINDA RANN, born in New Orleans, raised in Missouri and Virginia, has lived and worked in Texas since 1970. She earned her undergraduate and graduate degrees in Music Education from Louisiana State University in Baton Rouge, and has done additional work at Sam Houston State University, Texas Woman's University, University of North Texas, and Westminster Choir College.

Mrs. Rann currently directs five choirs and serves as Electives Department Chair at Dan Long Middle School in the Carrollton-Farmers Branch ISD, Carrollton, Texas. Prior to her tenure at Long, she taught elementary music classes with an emphasis in Kodaly and taught beginning band classes for one year. Her choirs at Long Middle School have been consistent sweepstakes winners. She has received the district VIP award for excellence in teaching, as well as the PTA Life Time membership award for outstanding service to school and community.

Mrs. Rann has over twenty years of public school teaching experience with emphasis in elementary and middle school vocal music, as well as ten years experience as Director of Music at the Lake Dallas United Methodist Church where she directs the adult Chancel Choir. Mrs. Rann is a frequent choral clinician and adjudicator. She has presented workshops nationally in the areas of middle school choral music and assessment in the performing arts. She is actively involved in state and national music education organizations.

ESSENTIAL ELEMENTS FOR CHOIR

A Complete Choral Experience for Grades 7-12

Created <u>by</u> educators <u>for</u> educators...a textbook to help choral singers achieve their full musical potential...<u>and</u> keep them in choir!

A two-faceted approach

The Repertoire...

ESSENTIAL REPERTOIRE
Choral Literature for Mixed, Treble, and Tenor Bass Ensembles
By Glenda Casey, Bobbie Douglass, Jan Juneau, Janice Killian, Michael O' Hern, Linda Rann and Brad White. Edited by Emily Crocker.

- High quality, time-tested literature
- Objectives based on the National Standards for Arts Education
- Historical, stylistic guidelines and cultural context
- Choral techniques (including warm-ups, exercises, and drills)
- Rehearsal and performance tips
- Assessment techniques and enrichment ideas

Essential Repertoire for the Young Choir (Recommended for Gr. 7-8)

08740070	Mixed/Student
08740108	Mixed/Teacher
08740071	Treble/Student
08740109	Treble/Teacher
08740096	Tenor Bass/Student
08740110	Tenor Bass/Teacher

Essential Repertoire for the Developing Choir (Recommended for Gr. 9-10)

08740111	Mixed/Student
08740113	Mixed/Teacher
08740095	Treble/Student
08740112	Treble/Teacher
08740115	Tenor Bass/Student
08740114	Tenor Bass/Teacher

Essential Repertoire for the Concert Choir (Recommended for Gr. 10-11)

08740116	Mixed/Student
08740117	Mixed/Teacher
08740118	Treble/Student
08740120	Treble/Teacher
08740119	Tenor Bass/Student
08740121	Tenor Bass/Teacher

Essential Repertoire for the Concert Choir-Artist Level (Recommended for Gr. 11-12-Adult)

08740122	Mixed/Student
08740123	Mixed/Teacher
08740124	Treble/Student
08740126	Treble/Teacher
08740125	Tenor Bass/Student
08740127	Tenor Bass/Teacher

ESSENTIAL ELEMENTS FOR CHOIR

The Method...

ESSENTIAL MUSICIANSHIP
A Comprehensive Choral Method
By Emily Crocker and John Leavitt

- Vocal technique
- Music theory skills
- Sight-reading skills
- Songs which encourage music reading
- Practical easy-to-use format
- One book works with all types of choirs – mixed, treble, tenor bass

Essential Musicianship - Book 1
(Recommended for Gr. 7-8)
08740069   Student
08740103   Teacher

Essential Musicianship - Book 2
(Recommended for Gr. 9-10)
08740104   Student
08740105   Teacher

Essential Musicianship - Book 3
(Recommended for Gr. 11-12)
08740106   Student
08740107   Teacher

For more information about *ESSENTIAL ELEMENTS FOR CHOIR*, contact your favorite choral retailer or write to:

ESSENTIAL ELEMENTS FOR CHOIR
Hal Leonard Corporation
7777 W. Bluemound Rd.
P.O. Box 13819
Milwaukee, WI 53213